Paparazzi

Book #3 - Evermore Series

By

Andrea smith

ANDREA SMITH

Paparazzi
Book #3 - Evermore Series
By
Andrea Smith

Paparazzi
by Andrea Smith
Meatball Taster Publishing, LLC.

Edited by: Ashley Blaschak Stout
Formatted by: Erik Gevers
Cover Design: Freya Barker

Dedication

This book is dedicated to my friend, Jennifer Stewart, who I playfully referred to as J-Stew the last time we talked, which was unfortunately, too many years ago.

Life happens. Good intentions to stay in touch go by the wayside, or are put off until *another* day in good faith that we have all the time in the world to make our connection. But the truth is, we only have now. Beyond that is not promised to anyone.

Jenny was the reason I started writing. We shared our love of writing back when we were neighbors, living our lives as 'desperate housewives' and dreaming of someday seeing our words in print. We devoured historical romance paperbacks and wrote contemporary romances together with strong female characters with sass - just like us.

I learned just recently that Jenny passed away in June of this year. I never knew she was ill; I never had a chance to say 'goodbye.' But that is the way she wanted it according to her family. Like all of life's challenges, Jenny was committed to doing it her way.

So, Jennifer, this book is for you. R.I.P my friend.

Re-Cap

To refresh the reader's memory, here are the highlights from Book 1 (Crushed) and Book 2 (Claimed) in the Evermore Series. Feel free to skip ahead if it's all still fresh in your mind.

In Book 1, "Crushed," we are introduced to Neilah Grace Evans, aged 13 when the story begins. Known as Neely, she has been uprooted from Tennessee when her father lands a job at a prestigious law firm in L.A., one that focuses primarily on entertainment law.

An only child, Neely has pretty much always had her own interests with which to occupy her time. That doesn't change once the family relocates to Malibu, California two years prior.

Seth Drake is fourteen when "Crushed" begins, and has been Neely's best friend from down the beach since shortly after her arrival. They swim in her pool, go to the pier to fish, hang out on the beach, and take the same school bus together.

The friendship eventually evolves into a first love situation between Neely and Seth. They enjoy one another's company more and more, and though they have distinctly different dreams for their futures, they find common ground in their present.

Seth's mother is an actress on a popular daytime soap, and Seth hopes to get into acting himself after college. That is his dream.

Neely, of course, wants to pursue her passion for art, specifically, painting in various medias, perhaps even becoming a teacher.

But things come to a crashing halt when Neely's mother starts drinking heavily, and the truth is exposed all over the tabloids that her father has been having an affair with a starlet, Tiffany Blume.

Her mother quickly flees California with her daughter in tow, hoping her husband comes to his senses and gives up the glitz and debauchery that comes with Hollywood.

It doesn't happen, though.

Her parents' divorce, and Neely finds herself back in Tennessee, away from her father, and from Seth, trying to pick up the pieces of her mother's life for her.

Fast-forward three years. Neely is now seventeen and has only visited California once since the divorce. That was the summer she was fifteen, and she spent a few weeks with her father.

During that time, things between Seth and herself heated up, but not to the point Seth would have liked. After a conversation with Laura, Seth's mother, Neely decided to cut her visit short. She left a break-up note for Seth, and returned the promise ring he had given her.

Now at seventeen, Neely has reconciled with her father after her mother enters rehab, and she finds herself once again in their home in Malibu.

Only everything has changed. Her father is now married to Tiffany Blume, and it is all Neely can do to remain civil to the glitzy actress. She has no desire to strike a bond with the woman who destroyed her family.

She has no clue where Seth is, or what he's doing, since she hasn't spoken to him for two years. She is determined to finish her senior year of high school and then find a college to attend where she won't have to remain under her father's roof any longer.

That's her plan anyway.

If she can just get through the next eight months without snapping off Tiffany Blume's head, she'll be out of there. She'll be on her way to becoming an adult, and carving a life out for herself. One that is free of the complications of emotional ties and family drama.

In Book 2, "Claimed," we find Neely back in Malibu, living with her father and stepmother as her own mother goes into a rehab facility back in Tennessee.

It's been a couple of years since she was last there, and Seth is studying at a Performing Arts college in New York City. Neely pretty much feels like a loner, and is biding her time until she graduates from high school and goes away to college. She's not fond of her new stepmother, and the same holds true for Tiffany Blume.

A chance encounter over the Christmas holidays with Seth on the beach has Neely's heart skipping a beat once again. However, she quickly learns that she misinterpreted Seth's intentions and is left feeling angry and humiliated.

Fast forward to her graduation. It turns out to be another 'night' to remember, but for all the wrong reasons. That night will haunt Neely for the rest of her life.

Chapter 1

April 5, 1999 (Present Day)

The night air was chilly and damp. Southern California wasn't supposed to host humidity, but here in the Valley, I suppose the weather played by its own rules. Just like every other fucking thing, be it animal, vegetable, or mineral.

My walkie-talkie squelched static, and then the crackling sound of Malcolm's voice came over. "Ten-six to nine, Cracker Jack."

Oh, puleeze.

Malcolm was my boss. And though he was a pretty cool guy, he did have this peculiar penchant for using police codes over the two-way radios, like exclusively. Oh, and if you were wondering, I am *Cracker Jack*. That's the code name I was assigned by Malcolm right from the start, which was going on seven months now.

"Ten-four to nine, Bald Eagle," I replied, switching the channel on my unit over to nine. He wanted to switch to a different channel for an extra precaution.

I still didn't understand why we didn't use cell phones instead of these contraptions, but Malcolm was adamant that going with walkie-talkies was a much more secure means of communication.

"Anyone can listen in on those damn cell phones, Neely," he'd argued when I nagged him for about the tenth time to lose the radios and get with the newest and easiest technology.

I snorted. 'Well, anyone with a two-way radio in the vicinity can hear our transmissions," I argued.

It was pointless. He wouldn't budge. "The beauty of it, Neely, is that nobody bothers with walkie-talkies much anymore. And besides that, we use code, so it's all good and we're keeping with tradition on this one."

It had been pointless to argue. This was Malcolm's business. He could run it anyway he saw fit. I was simply a Junior Operative, and part-time at that.

Oh, I didn't tell you, did I?

Malcolm West was a Hollywood private investigator. A one-man show, but that didn't mean he didn't pull the clients in because he did. He was as slimy as they come, but loveable as shit. I'd seen a 'Help Wanted' post on the bulletin board outside the Photography Lab at school when the semester started last fall.

Help Wanted - Part Time
Irregular hours, some night work, short notice.
Must have ability to take pictures and develop
them for private customers.
Must practice discretion and have reliable
transportation.
Call 555-3451 and ask for "Bald Eagle."

The post had creeped everyone out except me. I was intrigued, so I snatched it off the board and called. After my interview, I officially became Malcolm's part-time sidekick.

Most of the business coming into Malcolm's agency was from divorce lawyers in and around the LA area. And their clients were wealthy enough to spend funds trying to get dirt on their respective spouses in order to ensure the best divorce settlement possible.

Cheating husbands, cheating wives, scandalous public behavior, unsavory friends or business connections—you name it, we captured it on film. At least I did. That's where Malcolm needed my expertise. I had changed my major to Commercial Photography last fall, and I was always at the top of my class. My grades were mine, not the result of me doing my professor. Those days were long gone.

I pressed the button on the side of my radio. "Breaker one-nine," I barked, smiling mischievously. I enjoyed fucking with Malcolm from time to time, "What's your twenty, Bald Eagle? Am I gonna catch you on the flip-flop? Over."

I heard the crackling of the radio break, and then, "Very fucking funny, Cracker Jack. Your 10-62 has an ETA of seven minutes. Do you copy?"

"Ten-four. Out." I replied, shutting off the radio.

"Showtime," I thought to myself as I piled my hair up inside my ball cap, making sure the tiny camera that was made to look like a NASCAR button that I'd pinned on the front was ready and in place. It operated as a video camera and only had fifteen minutes worth of recording storage once I activated it.

I waited a few minutes, and then, sure enough, the Ponchello's Pizza car came careening around the corner, anxious to deliver before his thirty minutes were up no doubt. Same shit, every week for the past four that I'd been watching. People truly were creatures of habit I decided.

I pressed the tiny button on the backside of the pin and climbed out of my car, walking up the driveway where the driver was delivering the pizza.

The driver was leaning over, trying to check the order to see which pizza he was to deliver to the "Smith" house, I was sure. You'd have thought they'd have come up with a more original name.

Good. It wasn't the usual driver, which made my job easier.

He'd just slammed the passenger side door and turned towards the house when he spotted me coming towards him.

"About time," I said with a smile. "We're starving in here."

"I'm not past thirty minutes," he interjected quickly.

"Hey, I never said you were, Slick. Where's Jimmy? He's usually the one who drops off here."

He visibly relaxed a bit, seeing that I wasn't trying to jack a free pizza from him. "Oh, he...uh, had an audition or something. This is my first night on my own. I got lost for a minute when I got off Reseda. I think I'm still within my thirty minutes, but I got three more deliveries in the back."

"Well, here," I said, flashing him a smile, as I handed him a twenty. "Keep the change. I don't want to slow you down."

He hesitated momentarily. "You live here...at this address?"

I was still holding the bill for him to take. "Well...*duh*," I replied, giggling. "I just got off work. Mom had me order the pizza before I left so it would be here when I got home."

"Oh, okay then," he replied, grabbing the bill and shoving the pizza box my way. "Thanks for the tip. Enjoy."

"Drive carefully," I called after him and started up the driveway, moving a bit slower than my normal pace to allow him time to drive away. Once his car was well down the street, I prepared myself for Phase 2 of the plan.

At the front door of the one-story stucco ranch, I rang the bell and waited. I knew from previous stakeouts that our mark, Mr. Richard Blumfield, would be answering the door to pay for the pizza. My job was to see exactly who it was he had pizza with every Wednesday evening. The house was a rental in the Blumfield's secret LLC name, but it wasn't his residence, that much we knew. Movie directors with this guy's reputation didn't live in the Valley, trust me.

He answered the door, dressed casually in jeans and a sweater. Not a bad looking guy for being well into his forties.

"Right on time," he said, thrusting a twenty-dollar bill at me. "Keep the change."

"Thank you, Sir," I replied politely. "Would it be okay if I used your phone? That beater they gave me to use tonight died across the street," I explained, waving my hand toward Jazzy's vintage VW bug I'd borrowed for this assignment. "I have three more pizzas in the car, so I have to call back to the store to have someone come get me."

I saw the reluctance on his face and there was a moment of silence before he finally relented. "Sure, no problem," he said, opening the door wider, allowing me to step inside the house.

"There's one just around the corner to the right. It's on the wall right inside the door."

I followed his direction and stepped into what must have been the family room. A television was blaring, and across the large room, a fire in the stone fireplace crackled. An extremely pretty, and extremely pregnant Hispanic woman came into the room from an opposite doorway that led to the kitchen I presumed. She had plates and napkins in her hands, and a toddler followed closely at her feet.

"She needs to use the phone. Her pizza delivery vehicle broke down," Blumfield informed her. She smiled and nodded at me.

"I'll just be a minute," I promised, turning my back to them and lifting the phone from its cradle. I made a fake call to the pizza parlor, which was very convincing.

The toddler, as it turned out, was a boy named Luis. His mother was trying to get him settled into his highchair, and he was not a happy camper. He wriggled and squirmed, his little face contorted with anger. "Quiero Papá! Quiero Papá!" he squealed, his little hands fisted and flailing.

Su papá no se puede sostener, Luis, que está comiendo demasiado," his mother consoled him. "Y que quería otro, Richard? Lo que estábamos pensando?" she said with a laugh, looking over at the mark with love evident in her dark brown eyes.

He smiled up at her. "Éste es una niña. Probablemente se pegará a ti, María."

I pretended I didn't understand what was being said. This ought to do nicely I thought to myself, as they both turned to look my way. "Thank you so much. My ride is on the way. Enjoy your pizza. I'll let myself out," I said.

"Have a good evening," Richard Blumfield called after me.

Oh I would. I most certainly would.

Back at the office, Malcolm and I went over the video recording. "Does this tell us anything?" he asked abruptly.

"Of course it does," I replied with a sly smile. "I take it you don't speak Spanish?"

"Very limited knowledge of the language," he admitted. "Why?"

"Well, it seems our Richard Blumfield has a mistress with whom he's fathered a son, Luis, and has a daughter on the way," I replied, beaming.

"Bingo!" Malcolm said, holding his hand up to high-five me. "Well done, Neely. Mrs. Blumfield is going to be very pleased with your work."

Chapter 2

"Mr. Montego called you again...twice," Jazzy said, as I stepped inside our apartment. "Are you sure you don't want me to give him your cell number? You know, if you weren't so damn secretive about your number, we could get rid of the expense of having this landline."

"Yeah, yeah, you keep telling me that, Jaz. I cover the landline bill, so no worries."

She jumped off the sofa and headed into the kitchen. "I just don't get it, Neel," she continued, grabbing bottled water from the fridge. "I mean I know you're making good money, but still, if we pooled our resources and cut out some of the non-essentials, we could get a nicer place, you know?"

I sighed, collapsing down on our overstuffed sofa and hugging one of the throw pillows to my chest. "It will happen, Jaz, we're almost there. I graduate in five weeks with my Associate's Degree, and then I'm sure Malcolm will put me on full-time, at least I hope he will."

She plopped down beside me, taking a long drink of her cold water, "Is that what you really want to do?" she asked. "You're not going for your Bachelor's?"

I shrugged. "Not right now. I want to start making real money and do what I love: take pictures. Why not?"

She sighed, shaking her head. I knew where she was going with this. I could read Jazzy every bit as well as she could read me. I was waiting for her to follow up with her usual 'you're not meeting your full potential, Neely.'

"It's just that I don't think you're really living your dream, babe. You could make better money and take lots more pictures if you'd call Montego back, you know?"

There it was. Worded a little differently, but the same message rang out loud and clear. I chose to ignore the bait. I didn't want to go there. I grabbed the remote from the coffee table, and instantly powered the television on. "Shit, why didn't you tell me it was this late, Jazz," I bitched finding the station that hosted the show I watched every Wednesday night at ten o'clock. Only now, I'd missed twenty-two minutes of it, and had forgotten to record it.

Stupid! Stupid! Stupid!

"Oh for shit's sake!" she snapped, slamming her water bottle down on the coffee table. "You and that fucking show. I swear to God, I'm starting to worry about you. This...this obsession or whatever it is with Seth has gone on long enough, don't you think?"

"Shh," I hissed, "Wait until the commercial if you're going to bitch at me, okay? I've already missed a third of it."

She sighed loudly and got to her feet, mumbling something under her breath about me and my goddamn fatal attraction as she went to her bedroom, slamming the door behind her. It wasn't anything new from her. Jazzy really needed to refresh her script.

Okay, so yeah, I watched Seth's new show and even recorded the episodes on the VCR when I didn't forget to set the timer like tonight. What was so bad about that?

He had a starring role in *Bangor*. A big step up from his occasional appearances on Lotus Pointe, that was for damn sure. I was glad he'd left that show. I hoped with all my heart that it had left the producers in a lurch having to replace that character for the third time.

Bangor was pretty interesting. One of the few shows I watched religiously, and not just because Seth played the character, Robbie Spencer, the middle child in the family. His character had an older sister, Dee, who was a doctor, and a younger sister, Sally, who was a wild child. Their mother had passed away and the father was a veterinarian who practiced in the basement of their home in Bangor, Maine.

Robbie was kind of reckless, but in a non-criminal way which I found kind of endearing. He was twenty-one, the same age as Seth was now, and had a boyish, rakish charm. Seth fit the part perfectly in my opinion, and my eyes were glued to him each time he was in a scene.

I wondered if they really filmed parts of this in Maine. The scenery at the beginning was breathtakingly beautiful. It was a treat to see real trees that actually changed color in the fall. Not like out here. The contrast was refreshing, and it made me ache at times to go somewhere like Bangor, so I could see the lush autumn foliage and smell the crisp, clear scent of fall in the air.

I also liked the fact that, up to this point, Robbie had no romantic entanglements going on in the show. He was busy trying to book rock bands for the bar he'd just purchased, and working all kinds of hours because he couldn't afford to hire additional help.

I couldn't control myself. I would always keep tabs on Seth Drake. Part of me wanted to see how far his star would rise, the other part was just because I deserved the raw pain I felt seeing him every week on television, and knowing that he wasn't mine anymore. Maybe he never had been.

Jazzy referred to it as 'puppy love gone psycho.'

Whatever.

When the show ended, I immediately set the VCR to tape it each week. I stood up and stretched, a yawn escaped and then I noticed the scrap of paper with Jerry Montego's name and number scribbled on it still on the coffee table. As if there weren't a number of these placed conspicuously around the apartment from previous calls over the past couple of weeks.

Why wouldn't I return his call? It wasn't as if Jazz hadn't been nagging me to do so. After all, she'd bragged me up to Montego. She knew him from some club where wannabe cinematographers (like Jazz), camera, and boom operators hung out after hours.

Jazz was taking online classes and working now. She'd finished an internship last semester, and landed a job at the studio where she'd interned. She worked full-time and handled her studies. I was impressed she wanted to go on for her Bachelor's, but I knew I wasn't going to perfect my craft any more than I had by taking a bunch of frilly General Ed classes. I'd managed to complete the curriculum that fed my passion for photography. And that was what counted.

Jazzy wasn't exactly realizing her dream at the moment, but I applauded her determination. Right now, she was the right hand gal for one of the associate producers of a daytime soap. She said she'd do her time, make friends and connections, and eventually get where she wanted to be.

I knew she would. She had the drive and tenacity needed to accomplish damn near anything she put her mind to. I, on the other hand, was in a rut and I knew it.

I hadn't painted or sketched anything for what felt like forever. I had lost my motivation to do any of it. My muse was gone from my life.

Oh, that was bullshit and I damn well knew it. I had painted lots of different subject matter before Seth Drake had broken my heart the final time. Or had I broken his as well? Is that what we were? Two human beings with fractured hearts for no damn good reason?

But I had no real proof that Seth's heart had been broken. Just a look. One soulful look into my eyes that afternoon, when his beautiful eyes had flashed a kaleidoscope of turbulent emotions when the harsh words spewed from my trembling lips and landed between us. I'd even surprised myself.

Disbelief. Horror. Sadness. Regret. And finally, cold hard resolve. That was what I'd left him with that day. That was what I felt he deserved I supposed.

Now I wasn't sure.

I had every right to be angry and feel betrayed by the events leading up to my outburst, that much I knew. But maybe not entirely at him. It was him I had lashed out at because, in all of the drama that had gone down that afternoon, he had been the common denominator. But he sure as hell hadn't been the instigator.

It was water under the bridge now. Why did I continue to allow all of it to torment me? I hadn't seen or heard from him since, with the exception of his stints on television, or in the entertainment media.

Yeah, he was all over that and I was convinced it was God's way of punishing me for my sins. Of course, nobody *forced* me to watch *Bangor*, or to pick up the gossip rags that occasionally had his picture side-barred on the cover. Sometimes he was even with his latest flame. They always changed, and when they did, so did I. Thank God Jazz wasn't on to me there.

I ran my fingers through my auburn locks. This was a new color for me. I changed my damn hair color every time Seth changed girlfriends. I admit it. I wasn't sure why. I didn't probe my inner soul for a reason. I simply changed it to the same shade as his flavor of the month. People began to think of it as my signature *thing*, including Jazzy.

"Girl, I swear you're lucky your hair hasn't fallen out yet with all those home dye jobs you give yourself," she'd commented more than once. "Why don't you pick a color and stick with it for awhile?"

I didn't dare divulge my rationale for the recent change, because Seth had been seen and photographed by paparazzi at a New York bistro with Megan Call, an actress who had played a guest role on *Bangor*. Not as a love interest of Robbie on the show—no, she played some damsel in distress that had brought a dog she'd hit by her car into Dr. Spencer's veterinarian's office, freaking out with the comatose dog in her arms, and screaming, "Where's the doctor? This dog needs a doctor immediately!"

Seth's line had been, "Calm down. He's upstairs, I'll get him."

Were those lines enough to generate some Hollywood spark?

Maybe.

Or maybe it was simply two actors having a bite together, but I wasn't going to take any chances, thus the dye job. The fact that the paparazzi had been on it told me it was likely something more than just two colleagues having lunch.

PAPARAZZI

Fucking paparazzi.
Slime of the earth.
Bottom feeders, the whole lot of them.

I went upstairs and peeled my clothes off, grabbing clean undies and a tee from my dresser. I went to the bathroom and grabbed a quick shower. I had an early class in the morning and had about an hour of cramming to do before I hit the sheets.

Just as I pulled my bedspread and blanket back to climb beneath them, my eye caught a note that had been purposely left on my pillow.

Jazzy
Call Jerry Montego, Neely. He's the best and he wants
YOU, girl.

I sighed and went over to the dresser where my cell phone waited. She was right. There was no good reason not to call Montego, and I knew it. Then why had I avoided doing so?

I knew the reason, and maybe to most people, it was a pretty stupid reason. Most wannabe professional photographers having no more training and experience than I possessed would jump at the chance to be taken in by Jerry Montego. He was, after all, considered *big time* in LA.

And, it wasn't as if I hadn't met him before, although the circumstances for which that happened still left a dull ache in the pit of my stomach.

I stood there with my cell clutched in my hand and forced my mind to go back and replay that scene for the hundredth time in my head because I had to, at least one more time, before I dialed Montego's number. I had to see if I could at least try to shake the stigma of it all, because if I couldn't, there was no way I'd ever make this call.

Chapter 3

April 18, 1998

I've never actually been on the set of a television show. It's not as if Tiffany hasn't invited me like a million times before, but it's just never appealed to me.

Immediately after I arrive at the gate, I am taken by some shuttle service to the huge back lot that has rows of separate sound stages marked with numbers. They look like airplane hangars, nothing fancy from the outside. But next to the one we pull up to, there are several trailers lined up beside it. Apparently, those trailers are where the actors stay until they are called to the set.

I'm directed to Tiffany's trailer, where she's been anxiously awaiting my arrival. "Oh good, you made it. Come on, let's get you to wardrobe and make-up. You have a one o'clock call so we've got plenty of time to have them do you up nicely for your scene. Aren't you excited, Neely? Do you know how many real actresses would love to play this scene with Seth Drake...er, I mean Austin Benedict?" she asks, giving one of her schoolgirl giggles for effect. "I mean, yeah, you only have one line, but that close-up kiss? Plenty of girls in the business would do that scene for free, and you're gonna get paid!"

"Whoa!" I practically scream, stopping dead in my tracks, "Hold up right there."

She whirls around to look over her shoulder at me where I've stopped on the concrete pad outside of her trailer. "What?"

"You didn't say one damn thing about my having to...to kiss Seth!"

She looks genuinely confused, which is all part of her acting abilities, I'm sure. Not buying it.

"That was not part of this deal," I continue, not bothering to hide my anger. She has duped me on purpose. Whatever game Tiffany is playing is lost on me. To think nobody else could've fit the bill for one lousy scene seems ludicrous now that I've given it some thought. "You told me the scene is being shot with my back to the camera, you said nothing about a kiss. How could they even do a close-up of a kissing scene if my back's to the camera anyway?"

Then she got flustered. "Oh for heaven's sake, Neely. What is the big deal? You've kissed him before, haven't you?"

"That is not the point, Tiffany, and you know it! You deceived me on the phone last night. Why?"

She looks down at her painted toenails that are peeping through the strappy heels she's wearing. "Well, I thought you might not agree to do the scene if I told you that part, but really Neely, after all this time I don't see why you're acting like it's some big deal anyway. You have your back to the camera when you say your line. Then Seth moves in for the kiss. At that point, Camera 3 will zoom in from the side for a close-up, so the audience won't really see anything other than your lips pressed to his in a kiss. Then the A.D. will yell, "Cut!" and the scene is over. Then you can leave."

"I should leave right now!" I snap. "I can't believe how duplicitous you've been. Why would you do something like this to me, Tiffany?"

She starts wringing her hands in despair. "You can't go Neely, please, you just can't," she begs. "You see, I'm making my directorial debut on this season finale of Lotus Pointe. I know that doesn't mean anything to you, but it really is a big deal. If this falls through, I'll be in big trouble with the producers. Having experience directing is something every actor wants on his or her resume. It implies versatility in the business. This might be the only chance I get and I can't blow it. And your daddy, he was so excited and proud when I told him you agreed to do this. Please, I'm begging you; don't disappoint him no matter what you think of me."

Oh she just had to do that, didn't she? She's playing the Daddy card. Something tells me there's more to this story than what she's sharing with me. Is it possible her days on this television series are numbered? Maybe that's why she pitched this to me so passionately.

I give it some thought, trying to rationalize how this might be to my advantage, not withstanding disappointing my father. If Tiffany loses her role, there would be more financial burden placed on my father. In turn, it might have ramifications on his ability to foot my college tuition and I need to finish college.

She's watching me intently, chewing on her bottom lip. "Well, will you stay?" she asks meekly.

I sigh. "Yeah, okay. But I hope you don't have any more surprises in store today, Tiffany, because I swear to God, I won't think twice about walking off that set if you do. I don't give a damn about this show, about Seth Drake, or about your directorial debut for that matter."

She nods, but I don't miss the fact that her eyes have turned to ice. "I promise. No more surprises."

Two hours and ten minutes later she calls me to the set. The lady from wardrobe, Joanne, I think is her name, takes one last look and beams with pride. "Oh, you are quite exquisite in that dress," she says with conviction. "You do it more justice than Julia

Cantrell ever could. I swear I don't understand how she got that role."

"Wait—what?"

"Julia Cantrell. The actress who plays Cassidy Ryan—Austin's girlfriend?" she asks as if I should know all of this. "Don't you watch the show?"

"Nope. Never have."

And Tiffany Blume knows that very thing herself. Julia, the bitch from Seth's beach party, plays opposite him on Lotus Pointe. The BFF to Chloe for shit's sake! "Joanne," I say, "Is Julia the same actress who played Cassidy last season?"

"No, both of the characters were replaced by different actors this season. Tiffany Blume was instrumental in getting both of them these roles. I mean, she went way out on the limb for them. I don't like to speak out of turn, especially where show business egos are concerned if you catch my drift, but she sure was instrumental in getting that last actress who played Cassidy fired. Surprised me just how much power Ms. Blume has—" and then she stopped abruptly. "Oh I'm sorry, I forgot that she's your stepmother. You won't tell her I was running my mouth, will you? Dammit, I should know better than to open my pie hole like that."

"No worries," I reply and mean it. "I won't say a thing. We're not close."

"Come on," she says, holding the door open for me, "Let's get you on the set. You're gonna be just fine, Neely."

I don't share Joanne's optimism at all. This has all the characteristics of an impending disaster, but I will see it through somehow, if only for the chance to see Seth for the first time since the night of my high school graduation. Maybe it will help in some way to heal the wound I still feel pressing deep in my soul.

Joanne escorts me to the set and introduces me to a bearded guy named Dan who is the associate director she explains before leaving me there. I immediately look around; there is no sign of Seth yet. Tiffany is standing a few yards away, pointing to one of the multiple lights above and talking to a technician about changing the angle.

"Okay, so here's your line," Dan says, handing me a piece of paper. "Memorize it, and give me five to round up Seth."

I look down at the paper. Is he kidding me? It's only seven words. There is no memorizing to it. But the words. Fuck...the words.

Kiss me like you mean it, Austin.

Dear God.

I'm numb, but I'm furiously praying to the Lord above to not let it show. Seth and I are standing not more than two feet apart, waiting for our cue, I guess. The whole television set jargon is beyond me.

I can feel his gaze on me as we wait. It's penetrating and so far, I've not been able to return it. I busy myself with smoothing out my dress, checking the underside of my shoe, anything so I don't have to look into his eyes. If I look into his eyes, I'm a goner.

"So, looks like you've really gone a bit blonder since graduation, huh?"

Fuck. He remembers...that night.

I feel myself flush under his unrelenting gaze. I raise my eyes to his because he's not going to intimidate me with his good looks and his fame, I've decided. Nothing's changed. Everything's changed.

"You remember?" I ask quietly, so the set crew who are busy adjusting the lighting around us aren't privy to what we're saying.

His eyes study me as if he's placed me under his own microscope to dissect. "What, your hair? Or that night in the rose garden?" I see a flicker of amusement in his eyes. And it irritates me just a little.

I shrug as if I'm unaffected by his closeness and his words. "We were pretty wasted. I barely remembered it the next day."

He cocks an eyebrow and his mouth forms a thin line as if that offends him. "I was sober. I remember everything," he murmurs, an angry edge to his voice.

Before I have a chance to respond, Tiffany's voice rings out loudly, "Standby on the set!"

Seth turns from me and takes his starting position for the scene I've practiced a few times, with Daniel, sans the kiss of course, before Seth arrived on the set. I turn my back to Seth and find my mark. I'm supposed to turn and take three steps forward once Daniel says what he's supposed to say as the A.D.

Tiffany's voice. "Standby to roll tape!"

A male voice calls out "Speed."

Daniel moves in front of the floor camera with his chalk slate and pauses until Tiffany calls, "Standby Camera One on slate."

Daniel clicks the top down on the slate, and announces, "Take one, four cameras, common mark. Action!"

I take my steps, clasping my hands in front of me as Tiffany instructed earlier. Seth, as Austin, walks through the doorway, and immediately a look of astonishment crosses his face. "Cassidy," he breathes, stepping to his mark, which is right in front of mine, *"you came back. I've been looking all over town for you, baby. Don't ever run out on me like that again, do you understand?"*

His radiant blue eyes are gazing into mine as if he really means the words he's speaking to me, Neely, not Cassidy. And his hands reach for mine. As he takes them into his, I feel his fingers gently caressing mine, and he's doing it as Seth, not as Austin Benedict. My brown eyes are locked with his blue ones, and I'm feeling the current that flows between us with our connection. I nod like I was told to do so that he can continue with his next line.

"Don't you know how much you mean to me, Cass? Don't ever let someone try to tear us apart like that again. Now, if you don't mind, I have a need to kiss you."

I swallow. "Kiss me like you mean it, Austin," *I say with surprising sincerity.*

He moves closer, his face lowers to mine and my breath hitches as my eyes instinctively close and I tilt my face upward.

"Cut!" Tiffany calls out.

What the fuck?

Seth drops my hands and my eyes flutter open just in time to see the smirk on his face. "Anxious for the next part, Neely?" he asks. I have the urge to slap his smug face, but I don't. I have only myself to blame for my naiveté and stupidity. This is Seth performing. Nothing more. It's that...what did Blake say he used...oh, yeah. The Stella Adler technique. Probably the same technique he used the night Seth fucked me for the first time. I'm a fool.

Tiffany is now beside us. "Okay, so Camera 3 is going to roll in for a close-up, so make sure when Daniel says 'Action' you two give us some good stuff, okay? Your lips should already be together since the close-up will be right there. Seth, have your right hand tangled up in her hair so it shields her left cheekbone somewhat since she's standing in for Julia."

"Got it," he replies, stifling a yawn.

Oh, do I bore you, Seth?

"Great," Tiffany replies, giving him a smile. She turns and heads back to her director chair yelling, "Standby to roll tape. Quiet on the set! Standby Camera 3, read the slate."

Daniel holds up the slate, clicks it and says, "Scene three, take two, move to close-up," as I close my eyes and wait for the kiss.

"Action!"

Seth presses his lips to mine and I freeze. I don't know why, but I freaking freeze. They feel foreign. They shouldn't, but they do. I've felt other lips on mine since his, but none of them belonged to anyone that I loved, and yet, this feels so foreign and disconnected. My arms are at my side, and Seth continues to press his mouth to mine but there's...nothing. Just some anger welling up inside that is coming from who knows where, but I recognize that it is indeed anger.

"Cut!" Tiffany screeches, and she's on the set in five seconds flat. "What is that?" she asks angrily, her hands on her hips and her eyes on me. "You look like a fucking mannequin, Neely."

I back up and give her a glare. "What exactly do you want, Tiffany?" I hiss, "Our lips are touching, right?"

She sighs. "Look, Neely, your arms should be around his neck, like this, see? She grabs one of my arms and raises it up, wrapping it around his shoulder. "Now, can you do that with your other one?"

I don't care for her condescending tone one little bit. "You mean like this, Mama Tiff?" I ask, bringing out my Tennessee twang for her benefit.

Now it's her turn to glare at me, and it's a wicked one. I knew she had it in her to be evil, and here it is.

"Yeah, like that," she snaps. "You'd think you two never made a baby together with your stiff-as-a-statue posture, Neely. Now let's get this right on the next take. I'm not paying the crew overtime for one lousy scene."

She turns on her heel and leaves, but I barely notice because my mind has turned to thick fog with the words she just spouted. I'd run from this fucking set and out the door if I thought my legs would carry me. It's all I can do to stand here now and breathe. How did she know?

Seth clears his throat and spins me back around to face him. He's every bit as stunned as I am, but not for the same reason. "What the fuck did she mean?" he growls at me with flashing eyes.

"Nothing," I mumble, hearing Tiffany barking her set commands again. "Let's do this. I need to get out of here."

"No. We're gonna talk before you leave this set, Neely," he whispers hoarsely. "I mean it."

I nod, knowing that by agreeing, it will get this scene done and I can leave. I have no intention of sticking around and talking to Seth Drake.

We blessedly get through the scene and I'm still so numb I can't even recall what the kiss felt like when I get back to Tiffany's trailer and start tearing the dress off, grabbing my own clothes to hurriedly change, and get the fuck out of this place.

Someone bangs on the door of the trailer. And then I hear Seth's voice. "Neely, it's me. Let me in. I want to talk to you."

God no. I can't, I just can't.

I remain silent because I know I locked the door behind me. I finish dressing listening to him pounding on the door of her trailer, but I don't care. I know eventually he'll have to go back to the set for the next scene, and I can wait him out.

Ten minutes later, after the pounding has stopped, I lift one of the slates on the window blind and gaze out. He's gone. I breathe in a sigh of relief and grab my shoulder bag and head out. As I step around to the other side of the trailer, trying to locate a studio golf cart to give me a lift, I feel a hand on my shoulder, and I'm spun around roughly to face Seth.

"You're not leaving here until you tell me what the fuck Tiffany meant by that statement."

I pull away from him, but he's not giving up. He grabs my arm, trying to pull me back, and I scream for him to let me be.

"Talk to me, Neely," he pleads, the anger now dissipating from him. "Please, talk to me. Tell me what she meant."

"I don't know what she meant. You ask her if you're so damn curious. I don't intend to speak to her again." I was about to turn from him again, when his arms encircled my waist and he pulled me up against his hard chest. "What in the hell do you think you're doing, Seth?" I snap angrily.

"I'm kissing you the way you like to be kissed, Neely," he rasps, and then his lips crash against mine. "I'll kiss the truth from you, I swear it!"

And for a moment, I have no desire to try and escape from his embrace, because finally, it feels familiar again. I slowly melt against him, and my lips respond to his in an intimate and passionate way.

I can hear the buzz of activity from nearby, but when several clicks from a camera sound just a few feet from us, we both pull back to see who's encroaching on our private moment. The moment our faces are both turned in the direction of the camera, there is another click and then the man dressed as a craft services employee, jumps on his golf cart and drives away.

"Fuck," Seth growls, "Jerry Montego."

I turn to him, "Who is Jerry Montego?"

"Paparazzi...fucking paparazzi."

Chapter 4

Back to Present Day

I shook the memory of that day and what followed from my mind, at least for the time being. It was never really gone. It came and went, and probably would continue to do so for a long time to come. I had spoken only once since then to Tiffany Blume. I'd driven to my father's home and waited for her outside in my car.

My father had been in San Francisco on business that week. Tiffany hadn't rolled into the drive until after seven. She saw me before pulling into the garage. I had waited until she came out front again to exit my car.

"Why didn't you go on inside? You have a key, Neely. And whose car is that?" she asked, eyeing my 1988 Toyota with some disdain. But as usual, she didn't wait for an answer. "You know, I thought maybe you would have stuck around the set for awhile and watch the rest of the taping. I wanted to talk to you to tell—"

"Shut it," I said loudly, causing her eyes to widen with surprise. "I want to know why, Tiffany. Why did you set me up the way you did? What...what purpose could that possibly have served you, huh?"

She had remained composed. A smug look crossed over her face. "I didn't set you up, little girl. I was trying to do you a favor."

"A favor? A favor?" I asked incredulously, "How was that doing me a favor?"

"Don't you think Seth had a right to know?" She was fishing and I knew it. I remained silent, but my glare was toxic.

"You know, Neely, despite what you may think, I am not a stupid person. It didn't take a rocket scientist to figure out that you were pregnant what with the E.P.T. kit you left wrapped up in a brown paper bag, along with the test stick showing the positive results in the trash can in your bathroom. Not to mention that stomach bug you claimed you had last August before you moved out on your own."

My arms were now crossed in front of me, and I narrowed my eyes before I spoke. "Since when do *you* empty the trash cans around here, Tiffany?"

She scoffed at the question. "Don't be a fool. I don't empty the trash, but I sure as hell had instructions to the staff to go through yours, my dear. What with your mother's problems with booze, and the way you acted so withdrawn and those god awful things you painted on your wall...well, it was disturbing. I only wanted to make sure you weren't on drugs or something."

I hadn't believed what I was hearing from the bitch. As if she cared about anything other than getting what she wanted from whomever she wanted at the moment. She hadn't done any of it out of concern for me. "I'm really taken with your concern, Tiffany," I had replied, "but I don't believe a fucking word coming out of your mouth. What makes you think that test was even mine? Or if it was, that Seth had any part in it?"

She flipped her long blonde hair back over her shoulder and smirked. "Because, Malibu might as well be Mayberry with how fast things get around. Let's see," she continued, tapping her cheek with an index finger, "something about you getting drunk at a party and doing Seth in a rose garden. Am I close?

You just better be thankful I didn't clue your daddy in on your shenanigans. What'd you do? Get an abortion? Probably was best seeing how Seth has moved on to Julia—somebody who really is more suited to his lifestyle. Nothing against you—"

She never finished that thought because right about then was when the palm of my hand had landed with full force against her cheek with a loud smack.

It had caused her to go reeling backwards into the grass where she landed square on her ass.

"You are a spiteful bitch, Tiffany! You can tell my daddy whatever you want, cause I won't be back. But remember this: I owe you one." I watched as she struggled to get back up, and then I gave her one final smirk before I turned and got back into my car. I hadn't been back there since.

When my father had called me upon his return from San Francisco, raising hell with me for upsetting Tiffany, I told him that I preferred not to discuss it. He'd told me that I owed her an apology. When I'd refused, he hung up on me. A few days later, he'd called me back and apologized for hanging up. I told him that I understood he felt a loyalty towards his spouse, and that I wasn't trying to put him in the middle of anything. He'd asked me if I'd consider coming back so that we all could sit down and talk.

There was no way in hell that I was about to do that. I told him that maybe it would be best if Tiffany not be a part of the relationship between him and me. He wasn't happy about my terms, but it was non-negotiable from my perspective. And though we talked on the phone occasionally or met for lunch now and then, our relationship had been fractured, and I was sure that's exactly what Tiffany had hoped to accomplish.

I needed to stop delaying making the call I knew it was time to make. I pressed the numbers and waited until I heard a man's voice answer.

"Mr. Montego, this is Neely Evans. Sorry I haven't returned your calls before now. I hope I didn't wake you."

Chapter 5

Three Months Later

   July 5, 1999

I was crouching behind a shrub line next to the tennis courts of a huge estate on Mulholland Drive. Fourth of July weekend in lovely Malibu, California. My old stomping grounds. This was my first solo shoot, and I was determined I wasn't going to fuck it up by not getting the pic, or worse yet, getting busted for criminal trespassing. Jerry was testing me and I sure as hell wasn't going to blow it my first time out.

There was a big party going on. Loud music. Lots of people. Lots of drinking. Lots of coke being snorted. The more wasted they all got, the easier it would be for me to get close enough to blend in and not outed for the party crasher I was.

I unzipped the flap on my fanny pack and removed my 'EOS Kiss III' camera. This baby had only come out in April, but it was meant for what I do. Auto-focusing, thirty-five zone metering, and night lens photography. Plus it was compact. It only weighed three quarters of a pound with batteries.

I'd had a close call while climbing over the fence on the other side of the tennis court, after I'd disabled the security camera nearby. I'd learned a trick for that from Jerry. There's actually a way to disable those bad boys without it sending a signal to the security panel inside. It involves a squirt gun, some vinegar, a tiny bit of baking powder and—no, never mind. I really shouldn't be discussing tricks of the trade. I remembered Jerry had cautioned me against that from the start of my internship with him.

Should I back up? Did you miss it? I had a new career as of May 1st of this year. That's right.

I was now a celebrity photographer.

I am...paparazzi.

Yeah, Malcolm had pitched a bit of a fit, but I promised him I could freelance for his agency whenever my schedule permitted. He'd finally come around, wishing me the best and ensuring me that I was with the best for the career I was entering. I promised him it wouldn't be forever, because that was a promise I'd already made to myself.

I couldn't complain at all. The money, even during my internship, was pretty damn good. The solo money would be twice as much. Jerry loved it that I could process my own film as well. No worries that some PhotoMat® developer would scarf up the photo and make tracks to a tabloid before we got our pictures back, or worse yet, make duplicates and go to several tabloids.

"Don't think that hasn't happened before," Jerry had told me, thoroughly agitated. "Some people have no moral compass," he finished, shaking his head in disgust.

Jazzy and I had moved into a rental condo just off of Santa Monica Blvd. Yep, it was a real step or two up and we loved it, though it didn't come cheap.

Just then I heard some footsteps heading in my direction from the lawn. I peeked through the shrubs.

Damn!

Luck must be my middle name. It was my mark, and she wasn't alone. Everyone knew Devon Donnelly, the star of Primrose Place. Another nighttime soap that had hit the big time over the last few years. She was a femme fatale that loved the spotlight, and what she loved more than that was her wealthy husband's money and all that it afforded her.

Parties like this, for example, whenever he was directing a film in Europe. Yeah, she was married to none other than Truman Romanski, the most sought after director in the business. He was forty years her senior, but what he lacked in looks and apparently...dick, he made up for with his hefty bank account.

We'd caught wind that while Romanski was filming in Europe, Devon was playing hard and loose. Another photographer had caught her leaving the Hard Rock last night on the arm of her latest co-star, Ricky Havana, and had snapped some candid shots of the couple.

Problem was, Havana had broken the paparazzi's camera, and then his jaw. Whomever Devon was entertaining tonight wasn't Havana. He'd been locked up for criminal assault, and, as of two hours ago, even though his bond had been posted, the dude was refusing to leave the jail. Said he was going to make a political statement about invasion of privacy or some such shit.

Didn't celebs realize that with their fame and fortune came public interest—and even scrutiny? Whoever told them that fame was free?

Devon's soft laugh floated over the hedge line to my ears. They were pretty damn close it seemed, but they surely wouldn't be jumping the hedge. I peered through the branches and caught a better glimpse of the couple.

Devon was wearing a short, black jean skirt, with a white gauzy peasant blouse with billowy sleeves. Her hair was dark brown, and pulled up in a ponytail. Even in the darkness, I could tell she was wasted.

My eyes moved over to her male friend who had his hands buried in the back pockets of her jean skirt, trying to pull her back against him. She was squirming and giggling, playing coy apparently.

I could see his profile, and didn't recognize him immediately. He was tall, with a lean build, almost too thin to be what I termed "Hollywood Beefcake." His hair was jet black and longer than what was the current style. It wasn't until he spoke that I realized who the hell it was!

Oh My God!

Once I heard the way he talked, the British accent, and the words he used, I knew who it was! Jasper Knight, the front man for Maple Plaid. Maple Plaid was an up and coming combination new wave and rock band that originated in London. Knight's moves were better than Mick Jagger's, Steven Tyler's, and Bono's all rolled into one.

"Why did you want to wander out here, love? The party's back there, right?" his accent was enough to make me want to swoon.

I mentally chastised myself. I was on a mission here, and I needed to stop fan-girling, and do what I was being paid to do!

Devon giggled again, pressing herself back into him. "I needed some fresh air and some quiet. It was getting a bit rowdy back there, don't you think?"

I was careful to get my camera up to eye level without brushing against the hedges, which may have drawn their attention. They were close enough that I could smell the hint of Jasper's cologne in the night breeze. I started the recording. We could always get the best still shots pulled once we reviewed the film.

"You do have bedrooms in that monstrosity of a house back there, am I right?" Jasper said, his voice now husky, as he lowered his full lips and brushed them against Devon's hair. That would make a great still, I thought, my adrenaline pumping at just how close I was to this tabloid-breaking story. I was sure it would make the banner headline.

"Too many of Truman's servants in there with orders to watch me like their jobs depend upon it," she scoffed. "Give me a cigarette."

"Say please."

"Please?" she asked, acting put out by the fact she was showing manners.

"No, love, say it the way I like it."

She sighed and turned to face him, looking upward because of his tall stature. "Please, Jasper?"

He smirked and reached into the pocket of those tight leather pants and pulled out a pack of cigarettes and a lighter. He put two of them in his mouth and lit them, handing one to her.

"Thank you, Jasper," she replied dutifully, taking a puff as she pulled away and took a step away from him. It was then I noticed the bulge in his crotch.

Impressive.

Shit. Were they going to get it on out here?

Unfortunately, I would never know as just then her cell phone rang and she quickly tossed her cigarette to the ground. "I have to take this."

There was a brief pause, but I kept rolling the tape. I was hoping it was her husband on the other end of the phone, and she got into an argument with him right here within filming distance.

I watched as she suddenly stiffened and looked around at Jasper. "What? Are you sure?"

Pause.

"Okay, yeah. I'm heading back now." She ended the call and stuck her phone back into the pocket of her jean skirt. "Come on, Jasper, that was security. We need to get back up to the house. They're sweeping the property."

"What's going on? Party crashers?" he asked with a laugh. "Who'd you leave off your list, love?"

They started walking away in the direction of the mansion, but I heard her parting response to his question. "Not sure. Something about an uninvited guest being here. Probably paparazzi. I hate those fuckers."

What?

Shit! Had someone else weaseled onto the estate? Nobody was going to scoop me on these pics. I shut off the camera and placed it back inside my fanny pack and got to my feet. Just as I was about to turn and skedaddle towards the fence at the edge of the property, I felt a hand clamp down on my shoulder.

"Hold it there, Miss," a deep voice growled behind me. "Don't run off just yet."

Fuck.

Busted.

Chapter 6

I'd heard all about the fight or flight reflex, but this was the first time I'd experienced it full force. It seemed like minutes had passed instead of just mere seconds since the hand had been placed on my shoulder, and the masculine voice had halted my effort to exit the party.

It was me. I was the party crasher, and in Devon's terms, I was the fucking paparazzi whose presence had quite possibly interrupted a XXX porn scene between her and a major rock star. I wanted to kick my own ass.

I gathered my wits and turned to face my captor. The first thing I noticed was the embroidered shield on his black shirt that read "Security." There was no official law enforcement badge. He was private security. He had no jurisdiction over me, and I was about to blurt that very thing out when he spoke again.

"Neely? Are you...Neely...from the beach?"

I studied him closer, but he had a security cap perched on his head, and nothing really seemed familiar...until he pulled off the cap, and I saw the shock of red hair that tumbled out. "Remember now?" he asked cockily.

"Give me a sec," I replied, running a hand through my own hair. "Nelson? From Seth's party?"

"Right on, home girl," he said with a laugh, holding out his hand for me to high-five him, which I did enthusiastically with a sigh of relief.

"So, you're a *security* guard?" I asked, wrinkling my forehead, "I thought you were going into the business?"

He frowned, "Yeah, well that didn't work out so well. I'm back in college. I do this part-time to pay the bills. And speaking of careers, what the fuck are you doing here?"

I swallowed nervously. "Look, I was just fixing to leave, I promise."

He paused for a moment, his eyes moving down my body, landing on my fanny pack. "You know, I can't let you leave with that camera, doll. If and when those pictures hit the print, I'll be unemployed."

I stalled for time, my mind was working furiously. Could I outrun him? I dismissed that idea quickly when I saw his long, lean legs. "Listen, Nelson, this is my job now. My first solo assignment. Besides that, the camera set me back some serious cash. I can't leave it here. I need this job too. Can't you just say you didn't find me?"

He remained silent. "Tell you what. Some old busy body called over here about an hour ago and said she saw somebody climbing the fence when she took her dog out for a walk. I'm the only one on duty outside, so I'll report back that it was a kid that was already on the other side of the fence when I got here. But you have to make tracks, and you have to promise to never tell anyone I did this, got it?"

I smiled and nodded, extremely grateful for the break he was giving me. "Sure thing, Nelson," I replied. "And thanks."

"No, don't thank me, Neely. You owe me."

I looked back up at him. "I do?"

He nodded. "Seth Drake and Julia Cantrell did us both dirty. Did you know they hooked up? The son of a bitch stole her right from under me. Friends don't do that to one another."

I nodded. "Yeah. I heard."

"The way I see it is that it's really your fight, not Chloe's."

"What do you mean?" I asked, extremely curious as to how Nelson had come to that conclusion.

"It's like this. Seth had no interest whatsoever in Chloe. We all knew that he was into you. He might be a fine actor, but for those of us who saw him on a daily basis back then, we knew he was hung up on you. He used to mention your name enough, and how pissed he was about the way you dissed him. That whole scene at the beach was nothing more than a scene they did together for your benefit."

"My benefit? I...I don't understand."

"I mean they each were playing a part. To get to you, to exact some sort of payback for whatever the fuck you did to Seth that made him feel like he needed revenge I guess. I mean, shit, I don't know the particulars of it all, I guess you know that without me telling you. But I don't care what you did to him. It doesn't excuse the fact that a few months later he and Julia are doing a show together. And then, a couple of months later, she breaks it off with me. Tells me she's in love with Seth. What kind of a mother fucker would do that to a buddy?"

"You mean Julia and Seth are...*back* together?" I asked. "I thought they were done, I mean he's always being photographed with other chicks, I presumed that relationship was history."

He laughed bitterly. "They aren't *back* together, Neely, they're *still* together."

I shook my head and remained silent. My head was spinning with what Nelson had told me. I couldn't make heads or tails of what exactly I had done to Seth that would make him exact revenge, if that's truly what it was. Was this all about that stupid note I left for him? Or was it the fact that he thought I'd ignored the letters he sent to me afterwards which obviously, I hadn't seen until a couple of years later in a box in my grandmother's basement.

"So then, he's running around on her with all those other girls he's pictured with?" I asked, still confused.

"That's called *publicity*, Neely. Those are staged for the paparazzi. You're pretty new at this shit, aren't you?"

I sighed again. I couldn't deny that one little bit, but at least I was learning along the way. So those weren't girlfriends that I'd seen him with; that I'd changed my hair color for at all. Fuck me. So, it appeared a new hair color was in my immediate future. Back to blonde. "Apparently so," I finally answered him.

He let out a chuckle. "Don't feel bad. You know, I loved that girl, I really did. Even when she was in that car accident, I was right there by her side in the hospital. But it just didn't mean shit to her. I can guarantee you, Neely, the bitch will be cheating on Seth, too. Or maybe he will be cheating on her. Either way, when the time comes, I hope you're there to capture it on your camera. That's how you can return the favor."

I nodded to him, and I really felt sorry that not only had his heart been broken but one of his best friends had betrayed him in the process. That had to suck big time. "Don't worry, Nelson, if given the chance, I'll do you right."

"Good. Now get going so I can get back up to the house and report in. Be careful, girl. You're in a dangerous business."

Chapter 7

A few weeks later...

July 25, 1999

"Neely!" Jazzy screamed, as she barged out onto our deck at the condo, her eyes wide and a fresh copy of The Tattler in her hands, "Did you see this shit? Somebody scooped you, girl, and it made the front damn page! Look at the picture underneath the headline that says 'Knight Play while Hubby Away'!"

"What?" I sat up abruptly and feigned shock for her benefit. "Lemme see that!"

I pulled the paper from her hands and held it up to cover my face, because I knew it was going to be hard to hide my amusement from my best friend.

"Yeah, look underneath the picture. It credits some bitch named Grace Evangelista!"

I slowly lowered the paper downward towards my lap to expose the smile that was burgeoning on my face. She caught it immediately.

"What? You're not pissed?" she asked incredulously.

"Nope. Let me show you something." I reached over to the patio table and grabbed my purse. I pulled out a small silver case, and popped the lid open, pulling one of my new business cards from the top and handing it to her.

She read the card, and then snapped her head up to look at me. "You're...*her*?" she asked, confused.

"Surprise!" I yelled, laughing at her bewilderment. "You see, Jerry said I needed a cover name. This is a tough business, you know?"

"So, his name isn't really Jerry Montego?"

"That's right."

"Am I supposed to start calling you 'Grace?'"

"You better not," I warned. "This is a best friend secret. But in the press, I will be known as that and I'd prefer it if we don't make the connection public knowledge. In other words, Jazz, nobody can know what I'm doing for a living now. This is way different than when I worked for Malcolm even."

"And I kept my mouth shut then, did I not?" she asked, her hands perched on her hips. "No worries, my lips are sealed, girlfriend," she said chuckling. "But damn, you might've warned me! I was ready to put a hit on the bitch thinking she stole your thunder."

"Hey, you know this hit four major tabloids? Three in the States, and one in the U.K."

"Major bucks!" she squealed. "And I like the catchy headline there, Knight Play," she said laughing.

"Yeah, well I can't take credit for that," I replied, "Just the pic. But this is my step into the big leagues. I'm going to frame every pic of mine that gets published, along with the story. Is that too vain, though?"

"No way! This is your art, Neely. Why not display it at least for yourself since you have to keep it under wraps and all."

"I think so too," I decided. "Oh, and I'm going to be covering that after party next week after the Celebrity Golf Gala. Hope some kind of kink or drama goes down there."

"Honey, wherever there are celebs, alcohol, and drugs, you know damn well there's going to be some kink or drama."

She was right, and that was exactly why I was getting a real passion for my work. "I'm going as one of the catering party."

"Perfect. You'll be fine, but listen; I need to mention something here. You've gone blonde...like *again*?"

"Yeah, I did. You know, Jerry said it does help keep my true identity from being revealed. He encourages disguises, so I bought a shitload of wigs and hats. Wanna see?"

She nodded her head, and gave me a dazzling smile. "Sure, show me the goods. Hey, maybe I could do you up sometime?"

"Now *that* would be awesome," I replied returning her grin. "Maybe for my next gig, even?"

I so loved Jazzy.

I was sprawled out on our sofa, watching one of the *Bangor* reruns when the house phone rang. Jazzy had gone out to meet some of her friends from work, so I couldn't holler for her to get it and take a message. Yes, I realized I could pause the tape, but that simply interrupted my viewing pleasure.

"Hello," I halfway snapped into the receiver.

"Neilah Grace, is that you?" My mama's voice said through the other end tentatively.

"Mama?"

"Yes, it's me, Neely. It's been a long time, hasn't it?"

That was a fucking understatement if ever there was one. After not returning my letters, or phone calls to the rehab center, and then to her own apartment once she was released and got her own place, I'd given up.

"I'd given up on ever hearing from you, Mama."

"I can't blame you for that, Neely. I wasn't a very good mama to you, I know that, but I can do better, I promise."

How could I possibly respond to that? After almost three years since I visited her in that sanitarium, what did she expect me to say? "Are you doing well, Mama?"

"Oh, I am. I am doing just fine. How are you?"

"I'm good. Working. Living with my best friend, Jazzy."

"Well, that's nice, honey. I've got some great news for you, Neilah Grace. I'm getting married again!"

BOOM.

"What?"

"I'm getting married again to a wonderful man I met during one of my weekly Christian AA meetings. His name is Merle Jeeter. He's a widower. Four years sober, too."

I didn't have a clue as to how I should respond to that. My grandmother hadn't mentioned a thing about Mama having a boyfriend when we talked a month or so ago.

"How long have you known him?" I asked.

"Oh, you're just like your grandma," she replied with a laugh. "I've known him from AA group for more than a year. But we just started seeing each other about a month ago. He's a good man, Neely. I want you to please come out for our wedding. I want him to meet my baby girl!"

I was still trying to absorb the shock of what she'd told me. How should I feel about this? It wasn't that Mama didn't deserve happiness, but it all seemed so fast. I wondered what Grandma's take was on all of it.

"Neely? Did you hear me, hon?"

"Yeah...yeah, Mama. I heard. Well, uh...when is the wedding? I have to see if I can get time off from my job. I can't promise anything yet."

"It's August 10th at our church. But I'd really like it if you could fly in a couple days before that to help me get prepared. I want you to be my Maid of Honor. And Neely?"

"Yeah Mama?"

"Merle is a school teacher. But they're only human. I don't want you to think poorly of him for having kicked an alcohol addiction, you hear?"

"Of course. I understand, Mama. I wouldn't think poorly of anyone with a problem."

"Good. And one more thing. Don't tell your daddy. It's none of his business or hers."

"No problem, Mama. I'll call you in a day or two and let you know what my boss says about me taking time off."

I had no interest in going back and finishing watching the show. I had to play back the phone conversation I'd just had with my mother.

After three years of no communication, it was hard to believe that she hadn't asked me anything more about my life. Wasn't interested in what I did for a living, or if I had a boyfriend, or anything else. It had been all about her *good news*.

I picked the phone back up and dialed my grandmother. I had to get her take on all of this.

After I hung up from talking to Grandma, my suspicions were somewhat allayed. Grandma said while she did have some initial reservations about it being too soon, she couldn't deny the fact that Mama had remained sober and was going to church twice a week. I told Grandma I'd call and let her know my plans as soon as I knew them. I'd be staying with her, that much I knew for sure.

Part of me wanted to be happy for Mama, but the other part of me had some doubts as to whether this was going to do it. It was times like this that I longed for the ability to escape to the beach with my blanket and sketchpad and wait for my best friend from down the beach to come down to where I was and sit with me.

If things hadn't changed, that's where I would be right now. And just maybe Seth would be there, too. And we'd talk it out.

Together.

But together was ancient history, and maybe more of that blame was now on me than on him. There was no excuse for lying, no matter what the circumstances, but to purposely wound someone because of some selfish need to dish out pain, well, it was inexcusable.

Chapter 8

April 18, 1998

"Neely, you can't be sleeping with all that pounding on our damn door. Why is Seth Drake here? What the hell happened today?" Jazzy asked, sitting down on my bed where I've been laying in the dark since I returned from slapping Tiffany.

"You didn't let him in did you?" I ask, wiping my cheek.

"No, but he knows I'm in here. He saw me peeking out the blinds, now are you going to tell me what happened?"

"Later," I say, swinging my legs down from the bed and wiping my face. "First thing's first. This is my problem and I will take care of it. It's not fair to you or to the neighbors. We're not getting kicked out of here because of the racket he's making."

I go downstairs and wrench the door open, using my own Stella Adler technique, because I know I'm going to need it. "What the hell, Seth?"

He pushes through the door and whirls around to glare at me. "You owe me some answers, Neely. And I'm not leaving here until I get them, do you understand?"

He is towering over me, his hair is disheveled and my guess is that it's because he's been running his hands through it in frustration. Just like he always does.

He's never been so formidable as he is right now, and I know that he means every word of what he's just said.

I swallow nervously, silently cursing my evil stepmother for opening this can of worms for the purpose of what? Doing me a favor? How in the hell does this constitute a favor? She is a twisted bitch.

"I'm waiting, Neely," he says, his voice is cold and devoid of emotion except for maybe anger. But when I think about it, why should he be angry? I'm the one who was knocked up by our little tryst in the rose garden the night of my graduation. And, in all honesty, I don't know how it even happened.

"Okay," I say, taking a deep breath, "I was pregnant. It happened that night at the party. I don't even remember how it happened. You evidently took advantage of my inebriated state and had your way with me—"

"What the fuck is that supposed to mean? Don't you dare act like I took advantage of you, or like you didn't want it. You wanted it, Neely, trust me—you wanted it."

And that, for whatever reason, angers me. Not the fact that he'd said it, but because he knows the particulars and I don't. "So, you remember everything?"

"Every last detail. Want to know exactly how it went down?" he asks, cockiness dripping from his words.

"No—it's fine. So, we both wanted it, whatever."

"Continue, please," he coaxes, his voice softer now.

I shrug. "There's not much more to say. I missed a period. Felt sick in the mornings, so I suspected I was pregnant. I got a test kit and it confirmed that I was. End of story."

He stalks closer to me. He is too close. I can't say the rest if he stays this close, because his nearness is preventing me from saying what needs to be said.

His eyes drop down to my flat stomach, and then his eyes are back on mine. "Obviously, it's not the end of the story. It sure doesn't look like you had a baby back in February."

"Obviously," I snap.

He takes a deep breath, and I can tell that Seth is trying very hard to maintain his cool with me. "Why didn't you come to me, Neely? Why the hell didn't you tell me that you were pregnant?"

And his voice has gotten softer, and the anger seems to be dissipating from him. "I don't know," I answer honestly, "It was never a consideration. You'd made it clear you'd moved on."

There is a moment of silence between us, and I can feel that Seth is trying to choose his next words carefully. I know whatever those words are going to be won't be enough for me. How could they be? I'm just so close to losing it at the moment.

Stay strong, Neely. Be strong.

"You know," he starts, his voice gentle, "I hate that you had to go through that all by yourself. You should've told me, Neely. You should've come to me with this. It wasn't fair that you didn't. You behaved like a spoiled child with a secret."

I'm angered by his words. How easy this is for him to chastise me for not coming to him, when it's all in the past now. To simply presume that I'd had an abortion. My anger boils over because he doesn't know me at all. Before I have time to filter it, the words spill out of my mouth with venomous ease.

"I didn't want to come to you, Seth, don't you get that?" I snap. "I wanted to forget the fact that you had ever been part of my life. I wanted no reminder of you in any way, shape, or form. So, guess what?" I scream, "I handled everything myself without having to burden you with the problem. It was no big deal."

His face darkens with rage. For a moment, I consider that I've gone too far with my words, but there's no going back now. I see the tic in his cheek, and his nostrils flare as he stares me down.

"Glad to hear it," he replies, his voice is strained. "I guess you're right. Something like that is no big deal for a bitch like you,"

he snarls, turning from me and slamming the front door on his way out.

I release the breath I've been holding, and with that, the tears start rolling as well. I cover my face with one hand in shame. It's then I hear Jazzy's footsteps coming down the stairs in a rush. She is beside me in a split second.

"Why did you do that?" she asks, pulling my hand from my face. "Why didn't you tell him the truth?"

I shake my head back and forth. I don't answer her. I can't.

She's giving me a questioning look, while she waits for my response. "It just seemed easier," I finally sob.

"Easier? It's easier letting him think you had an abortion than telling him the truth? I don't get it, Neely. You wanted that baby, you told me so. Why couldn't you have been honest with him about what happened, huh? I could halfway understand it when he didn't know about your pregnancy. But he knows now. And that makes it different. Did you want to what, hurt him? Is that what this is about?"

"Stop!" I yell. "I don't want to talk about this right now. You don't know everything. You don't know what happened on the set or what that bitch of a stepmother did today to humiliate me, Jazzy. You don't know the whole fucking story of everything that has gone down between Seth and me over the years. It's...complicated."

"Then tell me, please," she begs, putting her arm around me. "Make me understand why you'd lie about something like that."

I nod. "I will. I'm so tired and beaten down, Jazz. I'll tell you everything that happened today. I...I don't know why I lied, but at the time, it just seemed like the right thing to do. It's going to be okay now. Seth hates me, and I hate him and maybe that's the only way I'll get him out of my head for good."

She looks at me warily. I know she's not convinced. And for the record, neither am I.

"Okay, Neely. Come on. Let's go to bed and we can talk. Everything will be okay, I promise. I'm sorry I yelled. You're right. I don't know the whole story, and I haven't been in your shoes. I'm sorry I jumped in your shit like that, forgive me?"

I nod and gave her a meek smile. "I'm glad I met you, Jazz. You're really all I have. And for the record? You can jump in my shit anytime you want."

And, like the best friend that Jasmine is, she climbs into bed with me and comforts me, as I cry off and on, while telling her all the secrets I've kept from her.

Chapter 9

Present Day

July 27, 1999

Guess who's getting married?" I said to Jazzy as we were making breakfast. She was leaning over the counter with her mug positioned directly under the coffeemaker so that she didn't have to wait for the glass pot to fill. Jazzy wasn't a morning person.

She yawned, shaking her head. "No clue."

"Mama," I replied, cracking an egg over the pan on the stove.

"No she's not," she said in disbelief.

"Yep. A teacher she met in her Christian AA group.

"Are you serious, girl?"

"I am. And get this, she wants me to be her maid of honor. Do you want bacon?"

"Forget the bacon, are you going back there?"

"I told her I would if Jerry gives me time off."

"You can't be serious, Neely. After the hell she put you through? Fucking with your life the way she did?"

Sometimes I wondered if sharing all of my secrets with Jazzy the way I had done had been a smart idea.

"She was sick, Jazz. She says she's better now."

"I'll believe that when I see it," she grumbled.

I had to laugh and point out the obvious to my best friend. "You've never even met her, so when do you think you will have an occasion to see it?" I asked, giving her a grin and hoping she'd drop the subject.

"No matter. I feel like I know her, and I see her through you…with what you choose to share with me. I just don't want to have to help you pick up the pieces again, babe. Just be careful, Neel."

"Yeah, I will. And I plan on asking her why she kept Seth's letters from me, too."

"Oh, speaking of which," Jazz started, "I have something to tell you. Blake called last night. He's back in LA. Guess where he's staying until he gets his own place?"

"You didn't invite him to stay here with us, did you? You know I have to keep a low profile—"

"Chill," she said, rolling her eyes, "Do you see him anywhere around here, girl?"

I giggled and felt duly sheepish. "Sorry."

"He's staying with Seth and Julia for now. Says he can hardly wait to find his own place. I guess they're a trip."

A trip?

"What exactly makes them 'a trip?'" I asked, part of me curious, the other part dreading the answer if it was something like them being so sickening sweet with one another that it gave Blake a sugar rush being in the same room with them.

"Argue all the time, I guess. Blake says there's so much negative Karma around them he's afraid it will rub off on him," she finished, laughing. "Anyway, he asked if I'd be his date for some party they're all going to next weekend in Malibu."

"Oh? Whose party?" I asked, cocking an eyebrow at her. My paparazzi instincts were kicking in hard.

"Some rocker. Alan Manzone?"

Some rocker?

"Are you freaking serious?" I asked, my voice booming with genuine excitement. "Uh, Jazzy, Alan Manzone isn't just some rocker, my God! He's...well, he's a freaking music genius on a hottie stick, that's what!"

"Hmm," she teased, "Sounds like someone's crushing on a rock star. I thought Jasper Knight was your wet dream gig?"

I sighed a bit in pure frustration. It was true. I had been crushing on Jasper Knight ever since my first assignment. There was definitely some kind of sexy pheromone he exuded with his mere presence.

But, in all fairness, I'd never been that close to Alan Manzone to see if he generated that same pussy-pulsing vibe. Alan was a bit older, way more famous than Jasper at this point, and an enigma of epic proportions.

As a fan girl, I'd loved to hump his leg if given the chance. As paparazzi? Well, it went without saying, I'd love to crash that party and let my camera tell the story afterwards.

"So, what exactly put Seth's crew on that A-List for one of Manzone's parties?" I asked, genuinely curious.

She scoffed at my question. "Seth's *crew*? Seriously, Neely, don't go there. There is no crew. Actually, it's a party to celebrate their newest music video. Blake did the lighting and Julia landed a spot in it. Seth's just going along for the ride."

BOOM.

Thud.

"I didn't realize Julia possessed that kind of talent," I remarked, knowing just how snarky I sounded, but also knowing that Jazzy wouldn't give a damn. No love lost there.

"When you have a daddy as well connected as hers, talent isn't always a priority. It's called quid pro quo. Besides, there are enough half naked dolls in those videos that nobody stands out except the band, which is really the point, right?"

"Mmm," I agreed, my mind going there.

"Oh please," Jazzy said, an evil grin making an appearance. "You're picturing Manzone's gyrating hips right now, aren't you?"

I nodded. She knew me so well. "And his bulging package too," I finished, feeling no shame whatsoever. "It's so sad that he's still living with Chrissie Parker. Lucky, lucky woman," I sighed dreamily. "If not for that, I'd totally do him."

Jazzy choked on her sip of coffee. "Listen to you!" she chided, laughing now. "You talk a game that you just don't play, girlfriend. Now when was the last time you *did* anyone, huh?"

She was right, but I wasn't going to give her the satisfaction of acknowledging her comment. "You'll have to tell me all about the party," I said wistfully. "God, if you only knew how much I'd love to be that close to Alan Manzone. You're living my dream, Jazzy," I finished, handing her a plate with her eggs and toast on it.

"I know what you're doing, Neely. You want me to offer you my ticket into that party, right?"

"Well," I replied, giving her a pleading look.

"Don't give me that puppy dog look; I could give two shits about the party. But I am curious, so answer me this."

I waited for the question I knew was coming.

"Is it because you want to get up close to Alan Manzone or is it because you want to watch Seth and Julia in action?"

I smirked. "Maybe a little bit of both," I answered truthfully.

Chapter 10

August 3, 1999
 Malibu, CA
 Alan Manzone's Malibu Mansion

"This place is beyond amazing," I practically shouted to Blake as we made our way through the throngs of people crowding the marbled hallway of Alan Manzone's sprawling mansion. I was actually referring to the artwork hanging throughout first floor rooms. I couldn't place the artist and it was driving me fucking crazy.

"Yeah, he knows how to throw a party for sure," Blake called back, as he led me by the hand through the maze of hallways and rooms that led to who knows where. He'd obviously been here before by the looks of his familiarity with the place. "It's a shame Jazzy's allergies flared up like that. I bet she's kicking her ass for having to miss this!"

"Oh for sure!" I answered as we passed a group of young women who were passing a pipe. "Where are we going?"

"To the patio. It's where the band is hanging. You want to meet them, right?"

I nodded and swallowed nervously.

We finally reached the great room where the back wall was entirely constructed of glass and revealed an epic view of the beach and Pacific Ocean beyond.

A concrete patio spanned the entire length of the back of the house. There were hordes of people surrounding the sparkling blue pool, filling the loungers and the clusters of chairs encircling the fire pits.

Blake took me by the hand, and pulled me outside, where my eyes immediately landed on Alan Manzone. He was reclined on a chaise, looking rock star chic, barefoot, flowing white shirt half unbuttoned, wearing snug jeans, and surrounded by people all fighting for his attention.

My pulse thudded faster with each step closer. Just being near him had infused my veins with heated excitement. I'd seen Alan Manzone before on TV and in magazines, but nothing had prepared me for real life Alan. He was that freaking gorgeous. Shoulder length tousled black hair, mesmerizing black eyes, perfect features, and a totally kissable mouth, walking the earth in six-feet of sexy perfection.

My cheeks burned—*kissable mouth*? Had I actually just thought that? And then I noticed Alan's potent midnight stare fixed on me as if he could read my thoughts and my legs faltered.

Blake laughed and leaned into me. "Don't go all fan bird on me. He's with his girlfriend. Not cool, Neely." Blake knew me better than that, but yeah, I was his beard so I needed to go with the flow.

My gaze shifted to the gorgeous blonde tucked against his side. Yep, it was her. Christian aka 'Chrissie' Parker. Hot bod, talented, and equally famous. Some girls get everything they want. First married to Neil Stanton, lead singer of Arctic Hole, and now Alan Manzone's lover. But she was exactly the kind of girl you expected the ultimate rock god to be shaking up with. And without really knowing her, I felt like I knew her well. And I liked her.

Their affair was epic and paparazzi gold. If only I could figure out a way to sneak a shot with my camera. It would be the biggest payday yet only because they were always so secluded it was difficult to get them together. At home. In love. Together.

How do I get a picture? How do I get a picture...

I felt the pressure of eyes on me and pushed away that thought because of the way Alan assessed me as if he knew my every thought even before they entered my head.

Unnerving.

My fingers tightened around Blake's hand as he maneuvered through the cluster around Alan's chair as though he belonged.

"Don't I know you?" I heard a heavily gravelly query and tilted my head to find Kenny Jones, Alan's drummer, sizing me up in a very obvious way.

Oh crap. Am I busted already? Help came from the least expected source.

"No, you don't, Kenny," countered Alan, rising from his spot, ignoring Blake's outreached hand and slipping an arm around him instead. Those penetrating, mesmerizing eyes locked on me. "Don't pay Kenny any mind. Worst pick up line in Malibu, love. He doesn't mean anything by it. It's his signature line. *'Don't I know you?'*"

Alan's eyes unwavering on me, he whispered something into Blake's ear I couldn't completely catch and they both erupted into laughter, Alan's low, raspy humor nearly caused me to fall on my backside as he finished. "...if you don't keep her close, Jasper's going to steal your bird for the rest of the night. Or haven't you noticed how he's checking her out?"

Jasper?

My heart jumped into my throat as I hunted through the crush of bodies around us for him.

"Not my bird to steal," Blake replied under his breath, causing Alan to laugh harder. "But you better watch out, mate. Cuz someone's moved in on *your* bird."

Alan arched a dark brow and stared down at his girlfriend in a way that was palpable and I knew in that second they were the real deal. All those stories in the tabloids weren't just overinflated hype to sell papers. They were crazy in love with each other. And when Alan Manzone's star aligned with Chrissie Parker's there were no distractions for either of them.

"Jasper, get the fuck away from my girlfriend, you wanker," Alan taunted, and my startled gaze discovered Jasper Knight on the spot beside Chrissie left vacant by Alan. "Come meet Blake's girl. Unless you want me to kick the shit out of you."

"On your best day you couldn't take me old man," Jasper shot back, smiling.

"On your best day you couldn't keep up with me in any way," Alan jeered, and they all laughed as Jasper sprang from the chaise.

Alan locked an arm around his neck in an affectionate guy hold. "Jasper, meet..." He paused, his dark eyes shimmering as the settled on me. "Sorry love, I don't know your name."

Jasper's gaze began to dance "The future Mrs. Knight," he supplied, shocking me with the boldness of his words that were equally matched with his stare. His accented voice ran through my body like a caress, and the way he gazed at me through his thick, sooty lashes totally unnerved me.

Alan released him. "Ah, so that's the way it is. Then why the fuck were you making the moves on Chrissie?"

Christian Parker rolled her eyes. "He wasn't, Alan. Every guy who talks to me isn't like you."

"They better not be, love," Alan chided, his black eyes shimmering, before he stepped back to drop a heated kiss on his girlfriend's mouth, leaving Blake and me alone with Jasper.

Blake cleared this throat, obviously noticing the way that Jasper Knight was making no secret of the fact he was undressing me with his eyes.

I flushed under his gaze—oh, not because of his eye fucking me. No, it was because he was clueless to the fact that I'd put his fledgling relationship with Devon Donnelly on the skids with the pictures I'd taken just a month ago. Jasper seemed to have bounced back nicely from the scandal.

Of course, he wasn't the one who had to put up with the Hollywood gossip that would drone on for months in Southern California. Rumor had it that Truman Romanski had put his young wife on a short leash after those pictures had hit the rags.

Of course, from Jasper's perspective, there was probably no such thing as bad publicity. Which of course, made me curious to find out why he was here at one of Alan Manzone's parties.

"Jasper—this is Neely. She's a friend of mine."

Nice Blake. How positively benign.

"Hey," I murmured, "Yeah, Blake allowed me to tag along. His *real* girlfriend is down with allergies you see."

Jasper snickered. "How unfortunate for her, but how fortunate for me, Neely. Would you care for a drink?" he asked, his hand moved to the small of my back as he urged me towards the table on the other side of the deck.

I whipped my head around to catch Blake giving me a wink and a nod as if to say, 'go for it.' I knew Blake was here for hob-knobbing purposes only. Doing the lighting for a music video certainly wasn't his lifelong dream, but it was a step in the right direction.

What the hell. I might as well make good use of having Jasper Knight's attention for a millisecond. "What'll you have, love?" he asked as we came up on the bar that had been set up complete with a hired bartender it appeared.

I didn't drink. I'd learned that lesson, but an occasional glass of wine was not out of the question. "White wine is fine for me. Something dry," I replied, glancing across the bar at the guy who was dressed in a black tuxedo, complete with white gloves and a top hat.

Oh. My. Fucking. God.

His look caused me to close my mouth swiftly, and I glanced away. It was Malcolm. My old boss, remember? He was on assignment. He had to be. I couldn't imagine business with his agency had dipped that low since I left to require him to moonlight.

I turned away from the bar and stepped over towards the stairs that led from the deck to the beach just as I felt Jasper tap my shoulder. I turned back, catching a look from Malcolm that clearly said, 'We'll talk later,' before taking the wine glass from Jasper. "Thank you," I murmured graciously.

"You like the sand and water, love?" he asked. "There's a volleyball tournament going on and a bloke whose teeth I'd love to knock out with my serve," he finished, laughing. Jasper had obviously been getting lit all afternoon.

"Not really. Why are *you* here?" I asked, and no, one sip of wine had not rendered me tipsy. I was simply curious, that's all. I needed to see where Jasper Knight fit in all of this.

Jasper tossed his head back and laughed heartily. "You get right to it, don't you love?" he remarked. "I might ask you the same if I hadn't seen you come in with Blake there. Are you his latest beard?"

"Fuck you," I replied, inching away from him. Fucking rockers. Think they can say anything to anyone. Fuck that. "Which married woman are you trolling for a fuck now that Devon's off limits?" I tossed back flippantly.

He placed his hand on my shoulder effectively halting my departure. I turned to face him and noticed his eyes were full of mirth. He hadn't been offended whatsoever.

"Whoa, hold on there, babe. I was just taking the piss. Truth is, I'm here because I was part of the video. That's right. I played a younger Alan, and during the tune, I morph into the current Alan. Hell, I've got to tell you, it was a rush and a half. I fucking love special effects. Have you actually seen the video?"

I turned back, taking a gulp of my wine. "Actually, no," I admitted sheepishly.

He gave me his dazzling panty-melting smile, and tugged at my hand. "Would you care to rectify that, love? I'd be happy to give you a private viewing."

I downed the rest of my wine and handed Jasper the empty wine glass. "Refill first, then let's do it," I replied coyly. Oh yes, this cat and mouse game was proving to be a refreshing distraction. I hadn't once considered looking for Seth and Julia.

Jasper returned with a full glass of wine with a cocktail napkin wrapped around the stem. "The bartender said you needed a fresh glass of wine. Said you left lipstick on the other one," he chuckled. "Asked if you'd mind wiping off your lipstick before drinking this one."

I looked up and over at Malcolm who gave me a slight nod. What was up with that? It wasn't as if he had to wash all the glassware, did he? I shrugged and turned to Jasper. "Lead the way," I said smugly.

My smug feeling of satisfaction was short-lived however once Jasper had seated us in Manzone's private theatre complete with leather recliner seats, walls that were completely acoustic paneled for sound perfection, and of course, state-of-the-art Dolby Surround Sound®.

He used the hand-held remote to dim the lights and start the video on the wide screen that ran the length of the wall. Immediately, my eyes landed on Julia who it appeared, had a starring role in this video. Fuck my luck.

Barely dressed, she shimmied and shook the best pair of tits her daddy's money could buy right in Jasper's (as young Alan Manzone) face. As much as I despised the bitch, I couldn't tear my eyes from the obvious chemistry that emanated between Jasper and Julia. I watched as they moved purposefully and seductively to the music, claiming the spotlight as if they owned this video and Manzone's band was merely a prop for them.

"Holy Mother of Christ," I murmured, louder than intended.

"We're hot, eh?" Jasper commented, his arm slipping around my shoulders, "She's got the moves, but I'm betting you've got some of your own, right love?" he finished, his lips so close to my ear that I felt his words more than I heard them. I shivered in response.

I knew what he was doing. I wasn't stupid. Aside from my obvious lack of sexual expertise having only ever fucked Seth and then Professor Andrews that one semester, I still knew a come-on when I heard it.

Jasper Knight was willing to fuck me because he couldn't fuck Julia. Seth was in the way. Probably the *bloke* Jasper mentioned earlier that he wanted to off with his killer volleyball serve.

But was I willing to let him fuck me? He'd been a crush I'd had but only in the abstract sense. You know, it was a star-struck kind of thing. I'd never really considered him anything more than a fleeting fantasy. In person, he actually was a letdown, if I were being honest with myself.

So why shouldn't I fuck him? I deserved to have some hot sex, and some celebrity sex would be a new adventure for me. All these confettied thoughts were swirling around my mind as Jasper's lips were now placing warm, soft kisses on my exposed neck.

I lifted my wine glass to my lips and took a sip. As I was lowering it to the cup holder I saw that I'd left lipstick on the rim. Oh fuck Malcolm, I thought. He'd get over it.

Jasper's lips were now moving downward, his warm breath tracing along my collarbone. "You smell so sweet, love," he murmured as my flesh tingled with anticipation. "I want to taste every inch of you. Would you like that?"

"Hmm," I purred. My hand found his cheek and I ran my fingers tentatively over his stubble. Was this really going to happen? Was I going to fuck Jasper Knight in the theatre of Alan Manzone's Malibu mansion? Was I that girl?

And as Jasper's teeth teased and pulled at my bottom lip, his breath now mingling with my own, I knew that yes, I was that girl. Why the hell not?

In the instant it took for Jasper to press the button that electronically positioned my chair to recline, I knew my decision had been made.

Chapter 11

Seth

She was here. I'd glimpsed her almost immediately from the sand where we'd been playing volleyball for the past hour and a half. Julia had insisted we play since she'd missed her workout at the gym this morning, but I also figured it was her way of avoiding Neely. Neely wasn't a welcome topic around our place. She never had been.

Blake had told us the night before he was bringing Neely to Manzone's party because Jazzy hadn't been feeling well. I hadn't been bothered by that fact nearly as much as Julia had. Maybe I had finally come to terms with everything Neely.

Or maybe I hadn't, I realized bitterly. When had Neely and I ceased to be important to one another I wondered.

Had it been when she'd left early to return to Tennessee that summer, leaving the promise ring I'd given her with a brief note telling me she thought we were both too young to make promises? I'd been devastated, but still determined to fix whatever it was that caused her to want to distance herself from me.

Or had it been when she ignored my letters and phone calls the weeks afterward, and then finally sent me the letter that had torn me to shreds?

Neely had been mine. Right from the start, even as kids before either one of us knew the score, I'd claimed her as mine. I thought she'd felt the same, but obviously, I'd been wrong.

I'd come inside from the beach to check out the party. I looked around and spotted Blake at the bar getting a shot of tequila from the looks of it. "Hey dude," I greeted, slapping him on the back, "where's your date?"

Nothing like getting right to the point about Neely and her whereabouts.

Slick. Real Slick, Seth.

He spun around, giving me a shit-eating grin that only meant one thing. He was shit-faced. "Uh...probably getting laid by Jasper Knight would be my guess."

I frowned. Was he serious? "What the fuck are you talking about, man?"

He tossed down his shot, and asked for another. "He took her to a private showing of the music video in the studio I guess. That was like thirty or forty minutes ago. You do the math." He waggled his eyebrows at me. I wasn't fucking amused.

For one thing, I'd had enough of the hype around the video. That's all Julia could talk about over the past month. Yeah, I got it that chicks had a thing for rock stars, but when she wasn't going on about Jasper Knight, then she was going on about Alan Manzone.

What the fuck was I?

Chopped fucking liver?

I had a starring role in a prime time drama series, not to mention that TV Guide had nominated me for a best supporting actor award in said series. And no, I hadn't won, but being nominated was no small thing.

"Do a shot with me, man?" Blake asked, bringing me back to the present. He held out a glass that had a shot of tequila in it.

"Sure. Why not?"

We both took a shot and I handed the glass back to him. "Hey, when Julia comes back from the restroom, tell her to stay put, okay? I'm ready to take off and I don't want to have to start looking all over the place for her. I'll be right back."

"Aye-aye," Blake said, giving me a salute.

I headed into the house and turned down the hallway that led to another wing in the mansion. I knew my way to the studio because we'd all been in there earlier when the video premiered.

Nobody was around, and when I reached the door to the studio, I noticed the light above it was illuminated to show *Recording in Process*. Yeah, I didn't think so since Manzone and the rest of the band were still outside on the deck partying.

I opened the door slowly, and peered inside the dark theatre. There was nothing on the screen, and no sounds were coming from the system with the exception of some soft static, meaning it was turned on.

That's when I heard another sound. It was the sound of skin slapping against skin, and a muffled, male voice groaning in pleasure. I froze just inside the door, my breath hitched in my throat. Somebody was getting fucked in here and I wasn't leaving until I knew who it was.

I silently descended the carpeted steps until my eyes were fully adjusted to the darkness. I could make out Jasper Knight's head and shoulders in the front row. His back was to the screen, which meant he was facing my direction, and had he raised his head, he would've seen me.

I could tell by his movements he was cock deep into pussy. And when I heard the soft mewling sounds coming from underneath him, my blood boiled with anger. That in and of itself took me by surprise.

What right did I have to be angry? I had no claim to Neely any longer. I was with Julia. Neely had every right to be with whomever she wanted. I was sure she'd been with plenty of guys since me. She was gorgeous and sexy, and had the most beautiful brown eyes that I'd ever seen.

All those thoughts were swimming in my mind as I walked down the carpeted aisle to see it for myself. I'd never allowed myself to picture another man fucking Neely. It was a visual I had no desire to entertain. But I needed to do this so at least in my mind, I could get past all of it. Maybe a shot of cold hard reality was what it would take for me to put the past where it belonged: in the past. None of these feelings or emotions belonged in my present. It wasn't fair to Julia. It wasn't healthy for our relationship. I needed to look forward and stop lamenting about things that could never be undone.

Jasper was so caught up in his pleasure, he never saw me approach. His longish dark hair framed his face, his eyes were closed, and his head tilted back as he rocked into her. I could see that her legs were wrapped around his hips, and her hands were clutching his ass, which was still covered in the denim of his jeans. He hadn't even taken his pants off. He'd just pulled his dick out through the fly and was pounding into her now. The fucker hadn't even bothered with a condom.

What the fuck was wrong with Neely anyway?

She was naked from the waist down, and I could hear the wetness of their fucking. My heart pounded in my chest, and my fists clenched at my side, wanting nothing more than to tear the two of them apart. To break between their joined bodies and make Neely come to her senses.

He'd made her wet. I hated that fact. It was a punch in the gut to me for some odd reason. Why was I still so possessive of someone that had never really been mine?

I was standing in the aisle, right next to the reclined theater seat where he had her buried down underneath his writhing body. They were both oblivious to my presence, only caring about the carnal pleasure each was taking from the other.

The scent of her pussy wafted up to my nostrils, and I felt them flare in raw, primal anger. I wasn't going to remain a voyeur much longer I'd decided, wanting nothing more than to snatch Knight by his long dark locks and pull him the fuck off of her.

Neely deserved so much better than Jasper Knight. Everyone knew what a whore dog opportunist he was. And just then she arched her back beneath him and clutched his pivoting ass tightly to her, letting a high-pitched wail escape from her lips. I froze in that instant. And then I just fucking lost my shit.

"You fucking whore!" I snarled, startling the both of them and essentially putting the kibosh on their impending orgasms for the moment.

"What the hell!" Jasper growled loudly, his eyes popping open and losing the heavy lidded lustiness they'd had only moments before. "Get the fuck outta here, mate!" he hollered, now up to speed on who it was that cockblocked him at the eleventh hour.

My eyes caught Julia's (not Neely's) horrified look as my words registered. "Gladly," I growled, my eyes locking with her frightened ones right before I spun around and walked back up the aisle and out the door of the studio.

I rounded the curve that led from the hallway into the large entry hall at the front entrance, and collided with a body. "Sorry," I muttered, not even looking to see who it was I'd nearly mowed down.

"Seth?"

I stopped abruptly and turned to look in the direction of the voice. It was Neely. Her brow knitted in concern or maybe it was confusion, I really couldn't tell.

"Are you...okay?" she asked studying me closely.

"I'm better than okay, Tennessee. I'm fucking fantastic. Thanks for asking," I snapped as I turned and made my exit out the front door.

I could give two shits how Julia was going to get home. All I knew was when she finally managed to drag her sorry, cheating ass through our door she'd find me long gone.

Chapter 12

One week later . . .

   August 10, 1999

"By the power vested in me by the State of Tennessee, I now pronounce you husband and wife. Merle, you may now kiss your lovely bride," the minister said. I watched as my new stepfather, Merle K. Jeeter, turned and brushed a fleeting kiss on my mama's lips. She was beaming.

"Ladies and gentlemen, family and friends, I present to you Mr. and Mrs. Merle Jeeter," the minister said, outstretching his arms to the handful of people in attendance. Besides Grandma and me, there was Merle's sister and brother-in-law and a few members of their Christian AA group.

Mama turned and took the small bouquet of carnations I'd been holding for her while they repeated their vows and she gave me a smile and a wink.

The organist began banging out the final hymn and Mama and Merle made their way down the aisle of our small church and out into the steamy August heat. I followed with Merle's brother-in-law, Grady, who'd served as his best man for the ceremony.

Such a small ceremony, hardly worth my trip back to Tennessee, but I had my own reasons for being here. And before I left to go back to California the following day, I would have some answers from Mama.

I'd been here for two days already, but with the flurry of preparations and the huge 'to do' list she'd given me, there hadn't been time to sit down and have the conversation we needed to have.

Merle seemed like a nice enough guy, and he definitely doted on Mama, which was exactly the kind of man she needed, but he always seemed to be at her side. And that fact hadn't given us much one-on-one time with each other.

"He's a bit overbearing don't you think, Neely?" Grandma had commented to me the first day I arrived and we'd all had dinner together. "Always taking charge, making the decisions for the both of them. I don't trust a man like that."

"Oh Grandma," I replied, "Maybe it's what Mama needs right now. God knows she wasn't making wise choices before she went into that sanitarium."

"I suppose so," she conceded. "Still, I'm not so sure hooking up with a fellow that has the same...*problem* that she has is such a wise idea."

I couldn't disagree with my grandmother on that one. I'd done a bit of research myself about the AA 12-Step Program. I'd wondered if Mama ever intended to get to the eighth and ninth steps. Because if she claimed she had when we had our talk, I was determined to call her out on it.

My opportunity presented itself the following morning as I helped Mama get everything packed for her honeymoon. Merle was taking her to Niagara Falls for a week.

"I just love the idea of a traditional honeymoon spot like that," she said. "Your daddy took me to Vegas, of all places, on our honeymoon," she muttered. "Nothing romantic at all about that."

"Mama," I started, sitting down on the bed, "I need to ask you something, and I don't want you to take it the wrong way."

She looked over at me from where she was standing next to the dresser in the room she had at Grandma's. "Well it sounds kind of serious, Neilah Grace. Should I stop what I'm doing for this?'

"You might want to," I replied. "Can you come sit here for a minute so we can talk?"

She nodded and her face became solemn as she took a seat on the edge of the bed.

"Now Mama, I know you've been in the AA program and I'm really happy that you've stayed on your path to recovery. In fact, I want to say how proud of you I am, because I know it's been hard for you these past few years. But I have to ask you something. Is there...well, is there anything you need to say to me? Anything you need my forgiveness for?"

She remained quiet, her forehead creased in confusion. It was quite possible Mama had no memory of things she'd done while under the influence, I knew that, but I hated to have to spell it all out for her. "I'm talking about Steps 8 and 9, Mama."

"I know that Neilah Grace," she snapped. "I'm thinking, okay? Look here, I know I wasn't always a good mother to you, so if it's an apology you're wanting from me, well you have it. I'm sorry."

She was acting kind of petulant now, and it pissed me off. "No, Mama, what I'm talking about are specific things you did that caused pain or suffering to people. Like these," I finished, standing up and going over to my purse and pulling Seth's letters from it. I handed them to her. "These letters that came to me from Seth. You never gave them to me. I didn't see these until Grandma told me about them a couple years back."

She looked at the envelopes now clutched in her hand, but remained silent. Her head lowered as if she felt ashamed. "I'm sorry, Neely. I did keep those from you, I admit. I was just so scared you'd up and leave me. I thought you'd go live with your daddy to be near that boy and I just couldn't let that happen," she sobbed, wiping her cheek with the back of her hand. "Will you ever forgive me, Neely?"

I nodded. "Yeah, Mama. I forgive you."

She looked up at me, her eyes still tearing up. "And that boy," she said, "I know I owe him an apology, too, but I just didn't figure I'd ever see him again, which I know, is no excuse. The things I put in that letter to him must've been pretty nasty. He never did write back after that," she continued, the sobs getting a bit louder. "Do you still see him, Neely? Or has he moved away from his mama too?"

"Wait. What are you talking about, Mama? What letter?"

She got up from the bed and walked over to the window so she was no longer facing me. "That second letter he sent to you saying he was coming to Tennessee and all. I couldn't let that happen. I knew if he showed up here, Mama would've felt obligated to tell him where we lived and then he'd show up there and convince you to go back to California. He'd see just how sick I was and tell your daddy to take custody of you," she wailed, wringing her hands.

"Mama, what did you do?"

She finally turned back around to face me. "I got on my typewriter and I typed him a letter. I signed your name to it.

And don't ask me what all it said, Neely, because I was drunk when I did it and I don't remember. That's the God's honest truth. I just know that it had to have been hateful enough so that he'd leave you alone. Leave us alone. Don't you see? I was sick then, Neely. I didn't want to lose you."

And then it suddenly all made sense to me for the first time. Seth's anger towards me. I had thought it was about that stupid note I'd left in his room. I was talking *note* and he was talking *letter*. A letter that I'd never composed or sent. But he hadn't known that; he still didn't know that.

"Oh Mama," I breathed, "you lost me anyway, didn't you? And it had nothing to do with Seth and everything to do with you and the choices you made at the time. And you were never going to apologize to me about any of it until I brought it all up today."

She rushed over to stand next to me. "Neely, you have to forgive me. I'm your mama and I was sick back then."

I shook my head. "I know, Mama. And the truth is, I will forgive you. I'm just not sure I can do it right this minute and mean it."

Her face fell and she nodded her head quietly. "I understand," she said quietly, "and I am sorry, for what it's worth. You tell that boy the truth if you have a mind to, Neely. And you let him know that I'm sorry for what I've done to the both of you."

Chapter 13

Three days later.

August 14, 1999

"Okay, spill girlfriend," Jazzy said barging into my room. "You've been holed up in here since you got back from Tennessee and I've got questions."

I was on my computer, checking emails, and responding as needed. I received an email from Malcolm with the subject line *Re: Manzone's Party*. I'd emailed him that I was back and would meet him at his office this evening so we could discuss the matter. I hadn't even clued Jazzy in on that before I'd left for Tennessee.

I turned my back on my computer and faced her. "Ask away," I replied with a grin. "The wedding was lovely. My mom's a shit. I'll most likely forgive her in time. Anything else you wanna know?"

"That I already knew. No, I want to know what the hell happened at that party! Blake's been all shady and quiet, and I know something went down that day because now he's crashing over at Jack's place. Seth apparently has moved to some undisclosed location, and it appears his relationship with Julia is over. Now, what the hell is going on?"

She was doing that whole eye bugging out thing, which was kind of funny, but she was dead serious. I didn't want to lie to my best friend, but I obviously couldn't tell her everything due to professional courtesy and confidentiality. I started telling her about Seth's near collision into me that day at the party, which was pretty benign information when her cell phone rang.

"Hold that thought," she said grabbing it from her pocket and answering it.

"What?" she shrieked, her eyes widening in shock. "Are you serious?"

Countdown.

5

4

3

2

1

"Let me call you back."

I looked over at my best friend as she broke out into a wide grin. "Pull up The Tattler's web page," she instructed, folding her arms in front of her.

I turned back to my computer and pulled it up. There it was. Front page, top banner. "Knight Moves On." And there was a picture, a bit shadowed, but not enough to hide the clarity of who the subjects were: Jasper Knight, lead singer of Maple Plaid and Julia Cantrell, television star from the hit series, Lotus Pointe.

"Hmm, great pic," I commented. "Looks like someone got a candid shot of something they weren't supposed to have seen. Why yes...there it is. Grace Evangelista."

"You beotch!" she screamed, grabbing my ponytail and giving it a hard jerk. But she was laughing and I knew I was forgiven. "You could have at least told me before it hit the rags!"

"Couldn't do it. I freelance, remember? I sell the pics. I don't guarantee they'll be published. In fact, some pics are purchased to *keep* them from being published. This one could've gone either way."

She scrunched up her nose. "Really? Well who bought this one?"

"Now that," I said standing back up and stretching, "is none of your business. I cannot disclose my client list to anyone."

"You know that just sucks," she muttered. "So, I guess that answers my question about Seth leaving. You didn't talk to him at the party at all?"

"Nope," I replied. "Not a word. It was a big party. Lots of people."

"Well, it looks like Jasper Knight gets around plenty."

"Yeah. Man whore that he is," I remarked. "Well, I gotta get ready for an appointment downtown. I'll see you later if you're going to be around."

"I'll be here. I wanna hear all about the wedding."

Oh. Fuck.

Not my favorite subject considering how I'd left things with my mother. But I knew Jazzy would be supportive of me on this one. She had never cut my mother any slack. And now I'd done the same thing after what she'd disclosed to me. I'd left without a word. And I didn't feel a bit sorry about it either.

"You got it, and oh Jazz?"

She looked over at me expectantly.

"You might want to share this article with Nelson if you run into him in the near future. He might get a kick out of it."

Malcolm had a shit-eating grin on his face when I walked into his office in Hollywood later that afternoon. I immediately held my hand out and was rewarded with an envelope stuffed with cash.

"My client was happy to pay for the picture, but obviously needed to sit on it for a week or so before deciding whether to go public with it or not. Either way, you got your five grand."

"Hey, you sure you don't want to take a cut of it?" I asked him. "I mean you're the one that clued me in on why you were playing bartender at Manzone's party that day. I did the easy part. You never were good with the camera though, admit it."

Malcolm laughed and sat down behind his desk. "I swear to God, Neely, I thought for sure those hidden video thingamajigs I was wearing would be failsafe. But with everybody hitting the bar every ten seconds the way they did, I didn't factor in the time I'd need to stalk the idiot."

"So," I replied, taking a seat opposite him. "You know, I can pretty well figure out who your client is in all of this."

"Have at it, but I will neither confirm nor deny. I keep my client list confidential, you know that."

"Yeah, well for fun let me give it a shot. Obviously, it wasn't Romanski, because if it had been him, he would've had you tailing Devon. Not that he probably hasn't hired someone to do just that, but she wasn't at the party. So, I'm betting Devon hired you to keep an eye on Jasper Knight. Funny how cheaters don't trust other people not to cheat isn't it? Such flawed characters I guess."

"Yes, they are," he replied with a chuckle.

"But what I don't understand is how you knew Jasper and Julia planned to hook up at Manzone's party?"

"Ah, I have my ways, Neely. My instincts are polished to perfection, you know that."

I didn't bother to tell him how close I came to being underneath Jasper Knight that day. If I hadn't insisted that Jasper go find a condom, I might never have lifted the wine glass to finish it off, and then seen the note scribbled on the cocktail napkin.

You're in my mix, Neely. Lose the Brit.

That was when the realization hit me that Jasper was the subject of Malcolm's undercover surveillance. Shit. I owed it to Malcolm to not fuck it up.

I'd scrambled to my feet and hightailed it out of the studio before Jasper got back. I actually had gone in a different direction so I wouldn't run into him on the way back. But once I realized I couldn't get back to the deck without going back down the hallway I'd come from, I cautiously retraced my steps. Right before I turned the corner in the hall, I'd heard Jasper's voice.

"What the fuck are you trying to do, Julia, and who assigned you the task of being my own personal cockblocker, huh? What'd you do, run her off?"

"I don't know what the fuck you're talking about, Jasper," Julia hissed. "And keep your voice down before everyone hears you. Are you stoned out of your mind again?"

"You don't give a flying fuck who hears me as long as it isn't that wanker you live with, am I right?"

"Please don't do this," she replied quietly. "I told you how it was with me. I have to consider my options."

"Oh, *your* options? While you chase mine away?"

"I'm not following you, Jasper. Can we go somewhere and talk about this quietly and calmly? You're not making sense."

But it was all making sense to me as I continued to eavesdrop from around the corner, a potted plant offering me the opportunity to peek around to see where they were without them seeing me.

Holy fuck. They'd been standing right in front of the studio door. I'd reached into my bag and pulled my camera out. Glad that the party seemed to be winding down and nobody else was in this wing of the house right now.

"Maybe I want to do more than talk, love," he replied cockily, his arm snaking around her shoulders and pulling her in for a kiss.

Great shot. I took it.

She pulled back. "Not here."

"Come on then. I know a place," he growled, taking her hand.

Another good shot. I took it.

And then they had disappeared inside the studio theatre. I'd discovered a back door to the studio when I'd gone down the unknown hallway earlier, trying to find a way back outside.

So, it served my purpose well to retrace my path and sneak back inside to snap a few more pictures from behind the darkened glass windows of the sound studio that was located at the front. They'd never known I was there. But I had been. And

I'd been there when Seth had quietly come down that aisle and discovered his live-in girlfriend having sex with Jasper Knight.

For some reason, I'd felt bad for Seth. But not so much that I was willing to keep the pictures of the couple fucking from Malcolm. I wasn't sure then what his mission was on this assignment. Therefore, it was up to him to decide what pictures to show his client. It wasn't my decision to make.

"We still make a good team, Neely," Malcolm said, bringing me back to the here and now.

"That we do," I agreed. "Hey, I like how you got that bartending gig. Great cover. How'd you manage that?"

"It's all about connections and I've got them. Bartending, catering, even housekeeping connections at some of the finer hotels in the area," he said with a sly wink. "Any time you need a cover let me know."

"Really?"

"Sure. And anytime I need some pictures taken or developed can I count on you?"

"Absolutely. Quid pro quo. That's us."

Chapter 14

Seth

Two months later.

October 18, 1999

My final appearance in this season's *Bangor* had finished shooting today. It was a wrap, as they say, for my character, Robbie Spencer.

It had come as no big surprise to me that my character had been written out of the series after my split with Julia Cantrell. After all, Glenn Cantrell was the executive producer of the series, so he had the power to call those kinds of shots.

He'd somehow blamed me for those pictures that got leaked to the scandal sheets. As if I'd had the presence of mind to take them or, at the very least, to have commissioned some paparazzi to do it for me.

What the fuck ever.

Grace Evangelista

That name seemed to be popping up on taglines all over the tabloids these days. Nobody knew she was coming until it was too late. Sometimes she'd leave her calling card behind, in which case, they knew it would only be a matter of days before a picture of them in some compromising position would be global news.

Some people would stoop to the lowest level possible to make a buck. Paparazzi were the lowest of the low in my book. Bottom feeders. Making their living off exploiting other people's private shit.

I grabbed my cell when it buzzed. It was Blake. He'd finally found his own crib and had been blowing up my phone to come over and check it out. It was down in Irvine, which, from Marina Del Rey, was about an hour's drive if traffic was flowing.

"Dude," he greeted, "What's up? You coming down for my house-warming party tomorrow night? And don't give me any lame excuses about spending twelve hours on the set. I know today was your last day, so a dual celebration is in order, right?"

I laughed, "Yeah, let's celebrate me being outta work. Why the fuck not?"

"Hey, it's not like you're gonna be outta work for long with that face, am I right? Enjoy a little down time why don't you?"

He was right. My agent was working on a couple of gigs already. She'd assured me I'd have at least one audition before month's end. And I did need some down time. I hadn't even finished unpacking since I'd moved here back in August. This was the perfect time to start reassembling my life.

"Sure, I'll swing by tomorrow night. It's nothing major though, right? I'm not up for anything loud and rowdy, Blake. I'm trying to simplify my life and keep everything chill, got it?"

"No worries, dude. Just a few of the people I work with at the studio. You know, I got my own crew now. Yep, I'm Chief Lighting Tech on *Lawson's Creek*. Moving right up. Oh, and maybe Jazzy stopping by to help me get my shit organized. You know, it needs a chick's touch and all."

"Yeah, okay. I'll see you tomorrow."

I grabbed a cold beer from the fridge and went to the second bedroom, which was being used at the moment as my computer room/office and dumping ground for all the boxes of shit I hadn't unpacked yet. I was determined to get them unpacked tonight.

No more putting it off. It was time to get organized and back on track. Fuck women.

I'd unpacked two boxes that contained all of my CDs, DVDs, and paperback books. I put them all in order on my entertainment center in the living room. The third box I started on had files, papers, newspaper and magazine clippings, and photos—stuff I'd packed up when I moved from my parents' house. I hadn't even opened it when I'd moved in with Julia.

I was leafing through it all, separating it into two piles: one to keep, one to toss. And then I came across *the letter*. I paused. It was going into the toss pile, but I couldn't stop myself from opening the envelope and torturing myself with her words one more time. Call me a fucking masochist.

I pulled out the typewritten page and unfolded it. Neely couldn't even have been bothered with writing it. She'd typed it to show just how impersonal it all was to her.

Seth,

You asked for a letter telling you how I feel? Well here it is. I don't give a damn about you and I never did. I'm so glad to be back home in Tennessee where the boys are gentlemen and not always looking to get down a girl's pants like they are in California! I told my grandpa not to put your calls through. But since you can't seem to get the message and keep writing these letters that I only tear up and throw in the trash, let me make it clear.

Don't come here! Don't call! Don't send any more letters! <u>I don't love you</u>. I don't even like you. I have a boyfriend at school that I love. He is way more handsome than you are, and he doesn't hassle me the way you did. He respects me. I never loved you, Seth. It was just a game with us. This is the real thing so leave me alone. I'm happy finally. I hate California. And you remind me of everything that was ugly and painful in my life. SO LEAVE ME ALONE!!!

Neilah

I crumpled the paper and envelope up in my hand and tossed it in the pile to trash. It doesn't stab at my heart anymore. But at the time, it had ripped me to shreds. I guess guys have first heartbreaks every bit as painful as chicks do. Well, most chicks maybe. Neely surely hadn't.

But I had carried that hurt in my heart for the next couple of years. The cruelty of her words had made me want to hurt her back. And when I saw her that night on the beach, I felt the hurt and anger surface once again.

So it being New Year's Eve, I partied for a while with my friends. Then, having some liquid courage coursing through my veins, I was still thinking about Neely and our earlier encounter on the beach. So, I decided to go down the road to her house. I knew she'd be alone, and I had every fucking intention of finally calling her out on her shit.

But when she'd answered the door, her hair all tangled and wild around her face from sleeping; her chocolate brown eyes searching my face in confusion, and the sexy little nightie that barely left anything to the imagination, I'd had no choice but to switch to Plan B. And of course, Plan B involved no talking, just dick action.

In that brief period when we'd sat together on the sofa and her scent had played havoc on my mind and my cock, I'd decided I needed to deal with Neely in another way. A more physical approach. So what the hell, we ended up fucking.

Only the thing was, it hadn't felt like fucking. It had felt like something entirely different. Yeah, I'd had sex since she dumped me, I mean, I was a guy after all, what would you expect?

But it hadn't been just the physical part of it—although, we were a great fit, there was no denying that. No, it was much more than that with her. It had been the emotions that surfaced each time she touched me; the kisses that we shared were familiar and perfect. The way her body molded to mine; her innocence, and yet the way she hadn't held back when she wanted to feel and explore every part of my body. She'd taken my breath away.

Once I was inside of her our bodies melded as one. I had been overwhelmed with the need to fully possess her. Our heartbeats were in sync and our breathing was shared and it was as if nobody else in the universe existed but the two of us at that moment.

So what had changed it for me? What had caused me to take the most beautiful experience I'd ever shared with another human being and demean it the way that I had?

It was when she'd announced she loved me. And I recalled exactly what those words meant to her because she'd told me in that letter. They meant nothing to her. This was just another game she wanted to play. Two years wasn't long enough for me to believe that Neely Evans had suddenly morphed from being a heartless bitch into becoming a soft and sweet woman.

So, yeah, I set her up at the beach party the next day. Played like I had a steady girlfriend with Chloe, who enjoyed assuming the role of the possessive girlfriend. The truth was, I hadn't set out to humiliate Neely. It was more about me wanting her to think that she'd been nothing more to me than a random fuck the night before. But Chloe and Julia got into the whole charade of being the designated *mean girls* that day and Neely had left practically in tears.

I shouldn't have felt badly for her, not the way that I'd laid my heart out for her two years before and she'd stomped on it with her hateful words.

But I hadn't quite counted on the fact that when Neely fled the scene in abject humiliation, I'd felt just as much pain inside for what I'd done as she had felt at the receiving end of it. And that was the moment I knew I still loved her. I didn't want to love her. I wanted to love anybody else *but* her, but the fact remained when she hurt, I hurt.

I'd thought for sure that would be the last we'd ever see of one another, and maybe it was just as well. Though getting her out of my head was never an option I learned. She was there to stay. But life went on and new distractions helped.

I busied myself with anything and everyone that would take my mind off of Neely Evans. It hadn't been easy. After the holidays, when her stepmother approached me about auditioning for a part on her show, I was tempted to turn it down flat without hesitation. My mother lectured me for an hour about opportunities such as that didn't come around often.

So, I auditioned and landed the part on Lotus Pointe. It was a perfect gig for me since filming wouldn't start until mid-July, and I could finish my semester of school in New York.

But then the night of Neely's graduation came around just as I returned from New York. I knew she'd be at Jazzy's party. It was no secret they'd become good friends. Blake had told me about it earlier in the day, and invited me to stop by to celebrate.

Against my better judgment and inner voice, I'd done just that. By the time I'd gotten there everyone was fairly loaded. Neely was nowhere to be found. Blake said that she'd gone into the hedge maze on a dare and hadn't come back out yet. Jazzy asked if I'd go find her.

It had been a setup that was for certain. So being the only sober person there, I'd gone in and found her in the garden area, flat on her back in the grass, trying to pull a rose off a bush. My mind drifted back to the details of that night.

"Neely," I say, "come on, let's get you out of here."

"Seth? What the fuck are you doing here?" she asks, sitting up quickly.

"Jazzy asked me to come find you and bring you out, now come on, stand up, and I'll help you out."

"Make me," she replies giggling. "Or better yet, do me."

"Stop," I warn as she gropes around in the darkness until her hands land on my crotch. For as drunk as she is, she has no problem lowering the zipper on my jeans.

"Aww, come on," she slurs, "Monty wants to come out and play, see?" She manhandles my erection like a pro. What can I say? I'm a dude. We like sex.

I fully intended to back away from her and get the hell outta there, I really did I swear, right up until the part where she put her lips on my cock. All bets were off at that point. She gave head like she'd been doing it her whole life, which I knew she hadn't.

In the darkness, the only light is coming from the stars and the moon, yet it's enough to watch her as she takes me fully into her mouth and swirls her tongue around the head of my dick causing my legs to feel wobbly and weak.

"Neely," I start, but then immediately forget what I intended to say after that. She is definitely taking charge of the situation.

"Lay down on your back, Seth."

I obey.

Still wearing my jeans, my erection is poking out from the open fly. I watch as Neely, dressed in a short jean skirt, reaches up underneath it and pulls her lace panties to one side and then straddles me.

*My hands brace her hips as she lowers herself down onto me. "God you feel good," she murmurs thickly, leaning forward so that our lips meet. "I'm going to fuck **you** this time, Seth. And for the record? Love's got nothing to do with it."*

I shook the memory from my head, not missing the fact it had made me hard. What was the point of rehashing any of it? It was time I accepted the fact that my stats with the female gender weren't impressive.

My last encounter with Neely had been at the Manzone party a couple of months ago. I'd practically mowed her down trying to get the fuck out of that house. I wondered if she'd found out what had gone down there with Julia and Knight?

Of course she had. It had been plastered all over the tabloids, but then I remembered Neely hated the gossip rags. She had ever since they'd outed her father during his affair with Tiffany Blume. She hated paparazzi because of that as well.

For me that shit was just a part of being a celebrity. A necessary evil. The price of fame. That didn't mean that paparazzi couldn't be useful when one used them to their own advantage.

My publicist, Diana Godfrey, had taught me that. It was, as she said, more troubling when one's name or face disappeared from the gossip columns. It meant they were old news or on a downward spiral. That was why she encouraged me to be seen on occasion with female co-stars in social situations.

She'd had plenty to say when the shit hit the fan with Julia and Knight back in August. "Seth," she'd warned me, "do not make any statements to anyone on this topic. Let them guess. You don't want anyone to think this actually bothered you. If you say anything on the topic, it'll be misquoted at best. Mum's the word, got it?"

"Yes, Diana," I replied, "I've got no desire to think about it let alone talk about it. No fucking problem."

And the interesting part was that aside from the fact I'd caught Julia fucking someone else and it had pricked my pride that was all it had done. I'd actually felt a bit of relief once the shock had worn off knowing it hadn't been Neely underneath Jasper Knight. My reaction puzzled even me.

I finished unpacking the rest of the boxes and then headed for the shower. Maybe tomorrow I could approach Jazzy in a discreet way to find out how Neely was doing.

I needed to know that she was doing okay.

Chapter 15

One day later.

October 19, 1999

"Are you sure you won't come hang out with us at Blake's new place?" Jazzy asked coming into my room where I was busy hanging another picture frame.

"I'm sure. I've got a gig this afternoon with Jerry. Need you to do my make-up before you leave," I reminded her.

"I know *that*," she huffed, coming up to stand behind me. "I'm not leaving here until six or seven. We've got time. I thought maybe you'd like to swing by later on. You're not working through the night, are you?"

"No, but I can't come by with my make-up and wardrobe still on, my cover, remember? Hand me the hammer," I continued, centering the nail.

"What you hanging up now, girlfriend?"

"My latest masterpiece."

I now had about ten major front page top banner pictures I'd snapped, framed, and matted with my name gracing the tagline at the bottom. The latest one was a candid shot I got while posing as a potential buyer of a beach house located next door to a superstar Hollywood couple. Since the showing was by appointment only, I had Malcolm show up about ten minutes into it as a persistent real estate agent from Encino who had the perfect couple interested in buying the place in order to draw the listing agent's attention from me.

I had thirty uninterrupted minutes to explore the property with my special long-range zoom lens camera in tow, which finally caught some great shots of one half of the Hollywood power couple.

"Is Jen pregnant?" Jazzy shrieked viewing the picture, her mouth now agape.

"I guess we'll know in time," I replied, gazing at the photo I'd taken that had been headlined and then bylined: ***Jen's Baby Bump****: Will there be an addition to the hit series Chums?*

"Well, from that position and with her wearing that bikini it does look like she *might* be expecting. Or it could mean she's been neglecting her crunches," Jazzy commented wryly. "I swear, when will the public leave that woman alone about procreating?"

I giggled, having totally wondered the same damn thing myself. "Probably when she's past menopause. Or maybe not," I concluded. "But hey, this pic landed me some major bucks. This is my Emmy in the world of tabloid photos!"

"Congrats," she commented. "But hey, what's your cover today?"

"I'm part of a catering staff for some engagement party gig in Beverly Hills. I have it on good advice my wicked stepmother is gonna be among the invited guests."

"Ooh," she said, flopping down on my bed. "How are you gonna get away with that?"

"You're gonna make me a guy," I replied. "My face will need some stubble, my eyebrows will have to go bushier. I'll need you to bind my boobs. I've got a fake moustache and a male wig that is killer. The rest of me will be covered with my white starched uniform."

"What about your hands?" she asked. "You have girl hands even if you don't believe in manicures."

"I'm serving food. I'll have to wear white Latex gloves. Easy peasy."

"This is gonna be fun. Let's get started."

Three hours later I was riding with three others in the catering van headed for Beverly Hills. Jerry was driving. I'd earned kudos from him for calling in a favor from Malcolm and getting us in the door at this particular event. We had to promise Malcolm a twenty-five percent stipend on any of our photos that got picked up by the papers or tabloids.

This was what we referred to as a smorgasbord event. There would be so many celebrities, politicians, and sports stars in attendance, it presented a plethora of opportunities to snap someone doing something news or gossip worthy. No press was allowed. Even ET had been shut out for privacy purposes.

You see this engagement party involved the daughter of a former sports legend. She was a well-known actress in a hit series, engaged to a professional baseball player who also happened to be the son of a former governor. See? A veritable smorgasbord of opportunities.

And the catering we were commissioned to do only involved desserts. So there would be a separate caterer for cocktails; one for appetizers and hors d'oeuvres, and another for the main entrees being served. It was quite an extravagant affair being hosted at the Soho Club in Beverly Hills. Our crew had been instructed to report to the club's personal pastry chef once we arrived.

My name tag read *Tony*. And I had to say, Jazzy had done a great job with my man make-up. "You kinda look like a geek, Neely. I did the best I could though," she commented almost apologetically as she handed me a mirror to check it out for myself. "I even gave you a scar, hope you like it," she said grinning. Jazzy's tenure at the studio had introduced her to several of the best make-up artists in the business. She'd picked up the skill, and was hoping to put it to use some day officially.

"Wow," I said, turning my head back and forth to see myself at every angle, "It doesn't resemble me, but I agree, I look like a dork. Scar doesn't help much with that," I replied chuckling. "Now for the finishing touch," I continued, grabbing the pair of black rimmed glasses I'd used before while working for Malcolm.

The glasses magnified my eyes, but did nothing to obscure my vision. All private detectives had a cache of this type of stuff that could easily disguise certain features. "What do you think?" I asked her once I'd slid the glasses on and turned my fact toward hers.

"Definitely a dork. But you got this," she said with a smile. "Wish I could be there to watch you in action."

We arrived at the club and the security guard cleared us to unload the van with the serving dishes, utensils, hot plates, and everything else that had been packed for the event.

The inside of the huge building was all art deco, and it was actually breathtaking. We met with the pastry chef and the event coordinator and got our instructions and location to set up.

Two hours later, everything was in full swing. Alcohol was flowing, food was being served, music was playing, and people were starting to loosen up. That was when I spotted Tiffany Blume. She'd come alone it seemed.

I hadn't seen my father in months. She'd succeeded in putting the wedge between us exactly as I'm sure she'd planned all along.

We'd tried doing the lunch or dinner thing by ourselves a few times, but that had tapered off once I'd started working for Malcolm and my schedule was so erratic. I hadn't even told him who I was working for then and certainly not who I was working for now. We talked on the phone maybe once or twice a month, but that was it. He hadn't even been to our new condo.

I was saddened by the fact we'd drifted so far apart, but the truth was, we'd never been all that close. Being that it was a Saturday afternoon, it was possible he was traveling back from somewhere, or maybe even out of the country. I wasn't privy to his whereabouts these days.

Tiffany was decked out in a low cut, black cocktail dress that clung to her every curve. Her hair, now tinted a darker shade of blonde, looked like she'd had it styled to frame her face in chunky layers. She was talking to a guy that looked to be in his early forties. Dark suit, stoic and very businesslike.

"That's Eric Fellner," Jerry whispered, coming up behind me to refill the crystal bowl of plain yogurt that I'd been tasked with dishing out. "He's controlling partner at Shooting Star Films out of the UK. Word has it she's vying for a role in his next film, *The Theory of Nothing*."

"Do tell," I said, now intrigued. Jerry knew there was no love lost between me and Tiffany Blume. And he knew I'd love the opportunity to catch a front page headline picture of the bitch doing something shady or ghastly. But so far, everything between her and this Eric dude seemed normal, though from where I was positioned, I couldn't hear their conversation. Their body language didn't betray anything other than casual business dialog.

Just then I saw him turn from her and walk towards the main hallway. She waited a couple of minutes as if she expected him back before turning around to where the desserts were lined up on the tables and headed towards them.

She slowly walked the length of the row of tables, not stopping at the assortment of pies and cakes, but acting like she wanted to. She finally spotted my yogurt and fruit display and moved towards it with purpose. She glanced briefly at her options.

"Oh Sir," she said, looking directly at my face and giving no sign of recognition. "I think I'll have some low fat plain yogurt with only a spoonful of the berry topping on it. No granola. And can you mix it up to make it swirly, please? Got to cut the calories wherever I can, know what I mean?" she asked with a giggle.

I nodded, loving the fact she had no clue who I was. "Yes, M'am," I replied in a deep voice, adding a bit of a Southern drawl to it. I dished it up for her. "More?" I asked, holding the parfait glass up for her approval.

She bit her lip and remained silent for a moment. It was if this was a major life decision tossed at her unexpectedly.

"Uh...no, I better not. That's fine. Oh, but maybe I will have one of those Biscotti's on the side?"

"Certainly," I replied, grabbing a dessert plate, I placed a paper lace doily in the center, and then put the parfait cup on top of it. I grabbed my tongs and placed a Biscotti on the plate next to the yogurt. So much pomp and circumstance for yogurt and a cookie, I thought to myself.

"Anything else?" I asked as the guy, Eric, she'd been talking to came back inside the room, his eyes searching it until he saw her in front of my table. He headed right over as if someone else might swoop in and grab her before he got the chance.

Interesting. Dynamics have changed.

"No," Tiffany answered. "That's just perfect. Thank you."

As soon as she turned her back to me, Eric was at her side, his hand brushing her elbow. "It's set. I changed my flight, and got a room at the Ritz. Room 712 say, in about an hour?" he questioned her quietly.

She nodded, spooning a bite of yogurt into her mouth, her tongue dancing along her lower lip. "I'll see you then."

It took me less than two minutes to inform Jerry of what I'd overheard. And another two minutes to call Malcolm to see if he had a connection at the Ritz. He did. Somehow I knew he would.

"Okay," Jerry said, "I'll take over here. They're going to be packing it up in about an hour anyway. I've got my eye on the governor's wife. She's in some sort of a snit with the bride's mother. They haven't said a word to one another, let alone gotten within ten feet of each other. They've got to do the toast together, so I'm hoping to get a good shot of them when that happens.

"But you need to beat a path over there now and get the lay of the land. This is award-winning photography. This will be big if we can pull it off, *Tony*," he said quietly.

I smiled and shrugged. "Grace Evangelista always comes through. Especially when it's up close and personal. Like this."

Chapter 16

Three days later.
October 22, 1999
Seth

I hadn't had time to put it all together in my mind until now. Three days after the fact and it hadn't really sunk in to my brain up until this point.

That was my fault.

It was this penchant I had for coming to conclusions after weighing the factors at play in any conflict I had to deal with in my own biased mind, and then neatly tucking them away where I'd never have to deal with them again unless I wanted to or I was forced to do so.

I tended to weigh the components as fact versus supposition a lot of the times, and that was based on my own personal judgments and opinions I'd adopted throughout my life. It made it easier for me to consider the outcome as black or white, good or evil, right or wrong. It was a flawed way of thinking I'd come to realize. And I came to that realization after Saturday night when I'd finally had the guts to ask Jazzy the question I'd wanted to ask her all evening.

But I'd procrastinated. Another flawed tendency of mine when in uncomfortable or unfamiliar territory, but hell, it was a perfectly acceptable human trait, right?

So, I had bided my time until well into the evening after we'd all partied for a while, and Jack and Blake left to make a trip to the deli and liquor store for eats and more booze. Jazzy had stayed behind to finish putting Blake's kitchen together, and I'd volunteered to set up his sound system in the living room.

His place was small, but nice. It was on the second floor and had a large walk out patio off the dining area. From the living room where I was setting up his sound system, I could see Jazzy walking back and forth between kitchen bar and dining room table where the boxes had been placed.

Jazzy had acted funny towards me all evening. We'd only seen one another in passing since the blow up I'd had with Neely over a year ago at their apartment. It was time to mend fences. I'd known Jazzy for a while. Not nearly as long as I'd known Neely, but still, I needed to start with her.

"So, you gonna hate my guts forever because of Neely?" I asked her point blank as her head was stuck inside one of the cabinets trying to maneuver the lining paper to fit.

She popped her head out and turned to me. "What makes you think I hate you, Seth? I might not like the person you've turned into over the past few years, but no, I don't hate you. I don't hate anyone. That's negativity I just don't need."

"Let's start with that scene that I know *you* overheard last year at your place. With me and Neely? It was ugly, I admit it, but please, hear me out."

"I'm listening," she deadpanned.

"Okay, well I was thrown for a loop that day on the set. Hearing that Neely had been pregnant and then her running out of there and refusing to talk to me about it, well that was bad enough. But the fact is when I finally did catch up with her at your place—the things she said to me were pretty fucked up, Jazzy."

"I don't disagree with you there, Seth. In fact, I told her as much."

That surprised me, but I continued since I had her attention and maybe even her support at the moment. "It wasn't even the pregnancy, per se, it was the fact that Neely hadn't thought twice about aborting the baby like it was some insignificant consequence of our lapse in judgment. She never once considered my feelings in the matter, or even felt the need to clue me in on it. She was selfish in every respect and that part is fucking unforgiveable to me. And maybe because you're a chick you can't understand that at all. But guys—well, guys have feelings too, Jazzy. Don't peg us all as being selfish pricks the way Neely did!"

She climbed down from the stepladder and walked over to where I was standing. "Are you finished now, Seth? Have you said all you needed to say about that, because if so, then I want you to listen to what I have to say."

I nodded, and crossed my arms, leaning up against the kitchen wall. "Go for it."

"Neely is my best friend. Even though I haven't known her nearly as long as you have, I know her inside and out. I know when she's happy or sad; mad, scared, confused, or any of the other moods she happens to be in at the moment. I know her heart and I know her soul because, you see, we share our secrets—good and bad."

She stopped. I figured she was waiting for me to say something. "Okay, Jazz—"

"Shut up!" she snapped. "I'm not finished."

Apparently not.

"For you to say those things you said to Neely that night last year was one thing. But for you to stand here right now and say the things you just said to me about how *you* feel wronged and how *you* feel cheated and how Neely was selfish in not considering *your* feelings—well, it's *so* fucked up that I want to plant my foot right up your self-righteous ass, Seth Drake! For as long as you've known Neely I'm here to tell you that you don't know shit about her! Get over yourself, Seth. And then do everyone a favor and either get over Neely or get the story right. That's all I'm gonna say about it—ever!"

She'd not given me a chance to react. She'd grabbed her jacket and purse, and flew out of Blake's apartment like a bat out of hell.

I'd scratched my head for about two minutes, and then I'd left too. And for the last couple of days, I'd replayed it over in my head again and again until it finally dawned on me. Jazzy was right. I'd missed the most important thing she'd said to me out of the entire conversation: *get the story straight.*

What the hell did that mean? What part of the story had I gotten wrong? I ran a hand through my hair and released a hard sigh. Had that been Jasmine's way of telling me I needed to talk to Neely again? Find out what part of the story I'd not understood?

Had I presumed she'd been pregnant by me, when in fact, it had been with somebody else? No. That part wasn't possible as I recalled the day on the set when Tiffany Blume had made that remark: *You'd think you two never made a baby together...*

I'd ripped into Tiffany Blume that day after Neely had hopped onto a passing studio shuttle right after the paparazzi had snapped the picture of us kissing.

Thank fuck the pictures had never surfaced, because by that time, Julia and I were starting a relationship. She would have been livid and rightfully so. To be honest, I wasn't sure what the hell had gotten into me at that moment, but whatever it was, it seemed to happen only when I was around Neely.

At any rate, I'd gone to Tiffany immediately and we'd had it out in the production office. She claimed she thought I'd known all about it. She said she thought it was the reason Neely and I had parted ways, and she thought by tossing us together in a scene, we might be able to patch things up.

What a lame fucking excuse for her apparent need to hurt her stepdaughter.

Once we'd finished filming the season, I told Julia I didn't want to renew my contract on Lotus Pointe. Her father was able to pull some major strings that landed me an audition for the new series, *Bangor*. He was one of the executive producers. Even Julia had thought it would be better for our relationship if we didn't work together. And me? I was just glad to be away from Tiffany Blume and her conniving ways.

The only way I was going to be able to put all of this to rest was to talk to Neely again. Get the whole story, the rest of the story, or the true story from what Jazzy had said when she'd ripped me a new one the other night.

I called Blake to get their address. I had free time for the next few days and I'd go to their place as often as I needed to until Neely was there and willing to talk to me like two reasonable adults, because that is what we were supposed to be now.

This thing—this wedge or negativity between us had gone on for way too long. It was kid stuff, teenage angst stuff, willful pride that went before the fall, but it wasn't us, not the way we were meant to be anyway.

It did not, nor would it ever define Neely and me and what we had been to one another for all those years. Yeah, I get that we were kids for most of those years, but the shit that really counted? The stuff that molded you into the adult you were destined to be? Well that was all determined in the formative years—and those were the years I'd spent with Neely at my side.

Neely and me swimming.

Neely and me on the beach, our feet buried in wet sand while we sculpted our masterpieces.

Neely and me fishing at the pier.

Neely and me skipping stones near our favorite hidden fresh water pond where the waterfall splashed over the rocks, and sharing our secrets and dreams.

Neely watching me run track and telling me I was the best even though I clearly wasn't.

Me watching Neely sketch and telling her she was the best when she clearly was.

Me walking Neely to her next class and frowning at any dude who dared to check her out along the way.

Me stealing a kiss or two while Neely painted a landscape in her backyard.

Me touching her for the first time in the front seat of my car in ways I'd never touched her before.

I'd been kidding myself thinking that I could ever be totally happy or fulfilled in my life without her being a part of it in some way. It didn't matter if we were friends or lovers, just as long as it was one or the other. She mattered that much to me.

I'd finally tossed her old letter in the trash because it was inconsequential in the grand scheme of things I'd finally come to realize. It was a very small part of the history that was us. But I'd stupidly allowed it to define Neely in a way I could never really see her and distract me from the truth.

The truth was I wanted—I needed Neely in my life in some way. I'd never felt for Julia the way I had for Neely. She'd been a surrogate; someone who was perfect for me *on paper*. But in the real world? Julia and I were both on a mission to launch our careers and I knew that by hitching my star to hers, my rise would be much easier because of her father and his influence.

It was pathetic, but it was the goddamned truth.

I checked my Rolex. It was just going on four o'clock. Neely might be out of class by now, that is, if she was still in school. I didn't know shit about her life anymore because I'd been so wrapped up in my own, and because I thought we were done with one another. But we would never be done and I knew in my heart she felt the same way.

Her eyes told her story. And that day this summer when I'd practically mowed her down I'd seen her eyes for a brief moment and they had told me everything I needed to know.

I mattered to her.

I always would.

The same was true for me with her.

I got into my car and started the route towards Santa Monica. It wasn't that far of a drive. Maybe twenty minutes. I would park in front of her condo if she wasn't home, and I'd wait for as long as it took until she arrived home and then we would talk.

I pulled into the 76 Station on Lincoln Boulevard to grab a soda and some chips in case it turned out to be a long wait. I hadn't eaten a damn thing all day.

At the register, I got behind a dude that was buying scratch-off lottery tickets, and then standing there and scratching them off to see if he'd won so he could collect or buy more.

I started whistling and tapping my foot, but he was undeterred. I glanced around and that's when the headline and picture caught my eye. The new Hollywood Tattler was out, and a picture of Tiffany Blume was plastered on the front with a caption: *Love Blumes at the Ritz.*

What the fuck? I could buy the rag and have something to read at least while waiting for Neely if I had to. I made my purchase and headed back to my car. I unfolded the tabloid to get a better look at the picture on front.

Holy fuck.

It was Tiffany Blume from the waist up wearing only a lacy bra. She was looking directly at the camera, her mouth hanging open in surprise—or maybe it was shock, and some guy identified as world-renowned movie producer Eric Fellner, with his face buried in her neck. He was naked from the waist up. My eyes scanned down to the photo tagline:

Grace Evangelista.

I started my car and pulled back out onto Lincoln Boulevard and couldn't help chuckling. Not that I approved of stalkarazzi, which was the category I placed this Grace Evangelista in being she seemed to have the goods on all of the scandalous shit going down in Hollywood, but this one felt good to even me.

PAPARAZZI

Tiffany Blume was due some Karma, and it looked like Grace Evangelista had served her up just that in a major way. I couldn't see Randall Evans putting up with that type of scandal, being in the business he was in. I wondered if Neely had seen this yet. I wasn't sure how she'd take it, but I knew she loved her father. I doubted whether that had changed.

When I reached the address that Blake had given me, there was one car sitting in the drive. I knew it was Jazzy's from watching her tear out of Blake's parking lot the other night. Hopefully, my arrival would show her that I'd gotten the message.

When she answered the door, her brows quirked in confusion. "Seth? What is it?"

"I want to talk to Neely. I want to get the story right. I'm kind of dense, I get it, but I'm here to make things right on that account. Is she here?"

Jazzy sighed and held the door open permitting me to enter. "You *would* pick today of all days to do this, right? Of course you would," she grumbled, closing the door behind me. "She's not here, Seth. But I know where she is if you want to find her. She'll be there for a while. And maybe it's the perfect place for your talk."

Jazzy had aroused my curiosity with her words. "Cryptic much?" I replied.

"Stay put. I'll get you the directions," she remarked, walking into another room.

I looked around. They had some pretty nice digs going on here. They must be making some decent bank to afford it. I knew Jazzy worked at a studio, but obviously, Neely was working now as well.

"Hey, she's not at work or anything is she?" I asked when Jazzy reappeared with a piece of paper in her hand.

"Nope," she said, holding out the paper for me to take. "She's there and she's alone. Just follow the directions."

I glanced down at the directions. "You're kidding, right?"

Her indomitable stare assured me she was not.

"Garden of Innocence Memorial Park...a *cemetery*?"

Jazzy nodded. "It's about thirty minutes from here. She'll be there until six o'clock when they close the gates, so if you wanna catch her, you better be on your way."

I knew Jasmine wasn't going to elaborate any further on this. So, I left and hoped that when I found Neely, she would be okay with my being there. It was so strange. But glancing down at the directions, there was a diagram of the section where Neely would be which told me Jazzy had been there with her as well.

Had her mother passed? Certainly Jazzy would've shared that bit of detail with me. I shoved a Metallica CD in and hit the I-10W towards Pasadena. I tried to relax as much as I could, knowing that at least I'd know the reason Neely was at a cemetery today, if nothing else, before it was all over.

Chapter 17

October 22, 1999

I hadn't been here in a year. This was the longest amount of time I'd gone between visits, but there was no way I would've missed being here today.

It was a sunny, balmy day, but then October in Southern California was usually mid-seventies with a light breeze. It was after five, so I knew at a few minutes before six o'clock the caretaker would be driving his pick-up truck through the paved driveway that wound all through the cemetery to make sure everyone left so he could close the gates.

The section I was in was usually deserted. Except for a few teddy bears placed next to a flower arrangement, or a balloon blowing in the breeze on a couple of the graves, that was about it. And those got to be fewer and fewer.

The first year, I'd come here more often. It felt like a place where I could reflect on anything and mourn in private without anyone trying to console me. Like Jazzy.

I knew before I'd moved out of my father's house that August that I was pregnant. My period had always arrived like clockwork, except for when it hadn't in June. And then again in July.

I'd informed Jazzy. Nobody else.

"Oh girl," she said, her eyes wide with concern, "What are you going to do?"

"What I'm not going to do is tell my father," I stated very matter-of-fact. "I'll be out of his house and in our apartment in two weeks so he doesn't need to find out."

"So, what? Are you going to get an abortion?"

I looked at her squarely. "I won't lie, Jazz. I thought about it, I really did. I mean, I'm the first one to stand up for a woman's right to choose, and I always will, but it's not for me. I considered it for about thirty seconds. And then I felt guilty as hell even for that."

She'd placed her hand on my shoulder. "I'm glad. We'll figure it out together. Are you..."

I hadn't let her finish. "No," I said abruptly. "I'm not telling Seth."

"No?" she replied, arching a brow. "Why not?"

"I can't throw a wrench into his plans. I won't do it. He's with someone else anyway. How pathetic would that look for me to walk back into his life with this kind of news, huh?"

Jazz and I had argued about that point on and off for the next few weeks. But she finally had backed off; telling me it was my decision and my life even though she didn't necessarily agree with it.

And so our life had continued on once we'd moved into our own place. I did all the things an expectant mother is supposed to do.

I saw a doctor.

I took my prenatal vitamins.

I abstained from all the things a pregnant woman is supposed to abstain from, not that I had been doing any of them anyway.

And I'd kept a low profile.

School and home. Home and school.

I kept in touch with my dad by phone, and had finally decided when I was in my fifth month of pregnancy, to share the news with him before the holidays. Even though I barely had a baby bump, I knew by Christmas it would be fairly obvious given my due date was February 24th.

We'd had plans to meet for dinner the following week. But, as it turned out, that didn't happen. I cancelled the day before telling him I was home with the flu. Besides that, there was nothing to tell him anymore. There would be no baby.

I stood up and brushed the errant twigs and dead grass from the flat marble headstone. A lone tear traveled down my cheek as I recalled that day two years ago when my heart broke for the very last time.

I read the words that I'd had engraved on our daughter's headstone.

Drake Evans
Born Silently Into This World
on
October 22, 1997
'Planted on this earth
to bloom in Heaven.'

I turned to look up as I heard a car stop and the engine shut off. I raised my hand to shield my eyes from the sun, knowing it was too early for the groundskeeper to be nudging me out.

When he got out of the car my breath hitched in my throat. He walked through the grass to where I was crouched down by the headstone.

Seth.

I was frozen. It wasn't in fear or in shock, it was more like I couldn't believe that he was really here of all places. How? Why?

It was as if he read my mind. "Jazzy," he said softly, coming up to stand beside me. "She told me you'd be here when I insisted I needed to see you. To talk to you. To get the story straight. I want to do that very much, Neely," he continued, dropping down into a crouched position next to me.

I remained silent, watching as his eyes left mine and traveled to the ground, and the shiny stone memorial that had been encrusted in that small piece of earth. It was the mark that told the world, or maybe just the handful of people that came to the baby section of this cemetery, or the groundskeepers that mowed around it that Seth Drake and Neilah Grace Evans had created an angel that would never walk among them. Not in this world anyway.

And it hadn't been insignificant. This tiny human being that had come into the world too soon, too silently, but not without a soul.

I felt another tear roll down my cheek, grateful that Seth had not looked back over at me yet when I heard his breath catch and caught the movement of his hand to his face where he cupped his jaw and rubbed his stubble.

"Oh My God," he said, and his voice cracked in a way that I'd never heard before. "Oh Neely," he continued now standing up and pulling me up with him.

Before I could even respond, I was wrapped tightly in his arms, and one of his hands was tangled in my hair at the nape of my neck, rubbing it softly with his fingers. He buried his face into my hair and pulled me in even tighter as deep sobs shook his body.

I'd never seen Seth cry. I wasn't sure up to this point if he'd even been capable of it. We were strangers to one another. "Why...why'd you let me think..."

"Don't," I said, my voice muffled against his chest. "Let's not do this, Seth. I'm tired of tearing each other apart."

I felt him nod against me. "Me too," he replied softly. "Me too, baby."

I wasn't sure how long we both stood there wrapped in one another before I heard the sound of the groundskeeper's truck. I pulled back from Seth, my hand wiped my damp cheek.

"We've got to leave, Seth. They close the gates at six."

He looked down at me, his lashes damp with tears. "Can we talk, Neely? No blame game. No rehashing shit. Just talk? I want to know what happened with my..."

He paused because he realized he wasn't sure if the baby was a boy or a girl. He waited for me to respond.

"Daughter," I supplied him.

He nodded and his fingers gently plucked a stray lock of hair from my face. "What happened with *our* daughter. That is, if you're up to it."

I nodded. "I am, Seth. As long as we don't make it about hurting each other."

He put his arm around my shoulders as we walked to where our cars were parked. "No hurt, baby, I promise. Do you want me to follow you to your house?" he asked softly.

My mind raced. There'd be no privacy there unless we went to my room. And if we did that, he'd see my shrine to Grace Evangelista and conclude that either I was her, or that I had an extremely odd fascination going.

"Um...can I follow you to your place? That might be better. Privacy and all."

"Sure, babe," he said to me. "I actually don't live far from you."

So, we each got into our vehicles and headed back towards the coast. I was prepared to share everything with Seth, but what I hadn't been prepared for was the way I'd felt again being in his arms.

It had felt right. Normal. The way it was supposed to feel between two people that loved each other. And no matter what happened, I would always love Seth Drake whether he liked it or not. I wanted him in my life, as a friend or as a lover, it didn't matter which, just as long as it was one or the other.

I never wanted to be at odds with him again. It was too painful.

When he hurt, I hurt. It was as simple as that.

Epilogue

Two years prior . . .

October 22, 1997

Jazzy was trying to keep it all upbeat for me. But there was no upbeat potential for this—there never would be. Not in a million years.

"So, has that epidural thing kicked in yet, Neel?" she asked, her leg doing that restless leg syndrome thing from where she sat in a chair across from my hospital bed.

"I'm not feeling any physical pain if that's what you mean, Jazz. But the contractions weren't that strong before anyway. I could've handled it all without an epidural."

"Yeah, you're tough, I get it. But why should you have to, I mean..." her voice drifted off.

"You mean why should I feel any pain when there's not going to be anything worth enduring it for at the end of this journey, right?"

"That's not what I meant," she snapped. "It's just that you've been through enough. With all that shit over the past couple of days with your doctor not knowing what the hell was going on with your...your..."

"HCG level," I supplied her. "And that could have been caused by several things, not necessarily anything catastrophic," I reminded her. "We didn't know anything until yesterday when the ultrasound showed that the baby had died in utero?"

"Yeah. Why didn't your doctor know there was something wrong?" she demanded.

"Jazzy, I don't know. Maybe it was something I did or didn't do. I didn't know anything was wrong so how could I expect him to know?"

"No! Stop that. You've done and not done everything you were supposed to, don't go there."

I nodded, taking a sip of my water. "I won't. But he told me we wouldn't know anything until after…after they do a post-mortem on the baby," I finished quietly.

The labor room nurse came buzzing into the room to check my monitors that flashed all kinds of digital and line graph data, which was Greek to me. "You're contractions are coming stronger honey," she said, patting my arm. "It won't be long now. Is the baby's father expected?" she asked.

"No," I replied. "He's not expected."

She gave me a meek smile and left the room assuring me she'd be back in a few minutes with the doctor.

"Why don't you call Seth?" Jazzy asked getting up and moving to stand next to my hospital bed. "He should be here."

"What would be the point, Jazz?" I asked incredulously. "I had no plans to make him a part of this baby's life, so why would I want to make him a part of her death?"

She looked at me. Stunned. "I can't believe you said that. Do you really think you're going to hold all of this together by yourself?"

"I don't have to. I have you."

She leaned over and brushed a kiss on my forehead. "Yeah, you do, girlfriend. You'll always have me."

An hour later, with Jazzy, the nurse, and my OB/GYN in attendance I delivered my stillborn baby girl. She looked perfect. Just miniature. She weighed fourteen ounces and was 8-1/2 inches long.

"Can I hold her?" I asked, as the nurse wrapped her tiny body in a baby blanket.

"Sure, honey. We'll give you a few minutes with her. The doctor has to fill out the Certificate of Fetal Death. It's required after twenty weeks gestation in California. You delivered at twenty-two weeks. So, I'll be bringing a form for you to sign with options for how you wish to handle the remains."

She hurried out the door before I could react to her last sentence.

The remains.

I was holding this tiny bundle that was still warm from my womb next to my heart and there was nothing inside of me that could think of her in terms of anything other than my baby.

My baby with Seth.

She'd been born silently, but she still had been born.

I pulled back the blanket and found one of her perfect little feet. "Look Jazz," I said in awe, "She has five perfect toes on this foot and, look here, five perfect toes on this one."

"I know, Neely," she sobbed, wiping at her eyes. "I know she does, girl."

"And look here," I continued, "She has peach fuzz on her head. Dark peach fuzz. I bet her hair was going to be dark like Seth's."

Jazzy nodded, another sob escaped her. "Neely, are you sure—"

"I'm sure," I said not letting her finish the question I knew was coming. "I can make the decision regarding her remains."

The nurse came back with the paperwork attached to a clipboard and sat down on the edge of my bed. "Now honey, most couples choose cremation for these little angels. So here's a paper explaining it all, along with several local crematories and their costs. The hospital will cover the cost of the cremation and turn it in on your medical insurance because it's covered. We will also make the call to the crematory for you so no worries there."

I nodded but my brain was officially in a fog. I was still holding my baby. It seemed somehow sacrilegious to be talking about the disposal of her tiny body with her resting in my arms.

"If you choose burial," she continued, "well that's more expensive, and here's all the information on that, along with the funeral homes in the county. Now if you choose to go that route, you will need to make those preparations and arrange payment on your own. The hospital doesn't handle those arrangements."

"I understand," I whispered, hearing Jazzy's sobs from somewhere nearby.

"Here's the Certificate of Fetal Death. This gets filed with the County Health Department, the Office of Vital Statistics. You'll need to sign it at the bottom."

I took it from her with my free hand and glanced at it. "Wait, this is wrong," I said abruptly. "This says 'Baby Girl Evans.' She has a name. I want this to show her name."

"Well, honey, you can put whatever name you want on her memorial. This is just for Vital Records."

"I know what it's for! And it's going to have her name on it or I won't sign it, do you understand?"

"Neely." Jazzy interjected, her voice trying to calm me.

"No," the nurse said, "it's okay. We can certainly change this for you. What did you name your daughter?" she asked, pressing her hand to my cheek in a gesture of consolation and compassion.

"Her name is Drake, D-R-A-K-E, last name Evans," I replied.

"I'll get this corrected and back to you then, Neely. You spend a few more minutes with Drake while I do that, okay?"

I nodded, cuddling my baby closer. I'd looked at the papers. There was no way she was going to be cremated. The burial costs were a little over two grand. "Jazzy," I said, "See if you can get someone to buy my car. I'll sell it for two grand, but I need it sold right now."

"Neely," she said, coming over to me, "your car is worth way more than that."

"I need to sell it right now. I've got a funeral and burial to pay for, so right now the price is two thousand dollars cash. The title is in my top dresser drawer at home. Can you get it and start making calls?"

And she did. Before the following morning my car had been sold and Jazzy had made the burial arrangements and memorial service for Drake Evans, my sleeping angel.

Four weeks later the post-mortem report had come back. Drake had died in the womb due to high HCG and ACP levels causing placental abruption.

It was an anomaly and was seen predominantly in first pregnancies. He claimed it wouldn't happen in subsequent pregnancies. It gave me little comfort though. The angel I'd carried for twenty-two weeks was gone. And no babies in my future would ever make up for the one that was missing.

ANDREA SMITH

THE END

Sneak Peek - Book 4
Star F*cking

November 15, 1999

"Look at this!" Jazzy yelled, barging into my bedroom before my alarm clock had even gone off. "It's here in the LA Times Entertainment Section, too. So it must be true!"

I sat up in my bed and rubbed the sleep from my eyes. "What the hell time is it?" I asked. "It's still freaking dark outside, Jazz."

"I don't know. A little after six I guess, but listen to this!"

She folded the newspaper in half and raised it up to her face. "Seth Drake, former star of the hit series *Bangor* has been cast in the lead male role in Samuel G. Barton's upcoming film *Love Plus One*, adapted from the best-selling novel of the same title. Drake will assume the role of Taz Matthews, the enigmatic special agent with the FBI, beating out several more seasoned Hollywood heartthrobs such as Leo Caprialo, Luke Jeffries, and Dash Ervin. The casting hasn't been completed yet for the female lead, however it has been widely speculated that competing for the role of Lindsey Dennison is one of the "Emmas," one of the "Emilys," and two of the "Ashleys." Oh for Chrissake, can they be any more cryptic?" Jazzy huffed. "I mean which one of the Emmas, Emilys or Ashleys? There are like five each! Anyway, the movie deal stands to put Drake on the A-List of male leads going forward and his earnings from the movie will certainly net him a seven-figure take home!"

Jazzy was jumping up and down like a kid at Christmas. She finally stopped, and whirled around to look at me.

I was sitting in my bed, yawning, and giving her the stink eye for waking me up this damn early. I'd gotten in late last night from Seth's place, and had an early appointment this morning in LA with Jerry.

"Aren't you even excited?" she asked, looking at me like I had grown two heads or something.

"Yeah, Jazz, but I already knew about it. He told me last night and I had every intention of sharing it with you this morning. Once I woke up and had my mug of coffee in front of me and maybe a toasted bagel and a glass of juice? Like when we sit across the table from each other and have breakfast and conversation together some mornings? The way reasonable people do?"

I plopped back down on my bed and pulled my covers up to my chin. "But, once again, I see the LA Times has beaten me to the punch. Stolen my thunder, if you will. So now you know and I think I'll go back to sleep for a little bit, 'kay?"

"Oh...*you*!" she hollered, tackling me on the bed. "You could've woken my ass up with this news last night and I sure as hell wouldn't have gone all psycho bitch on you, you know?"

"Oh, yeah, right!" I screamed and giggled as we both started bitch-wrestling with one another.

"So, you gonna tell me how things are these days between you and your superstar?" she asked, giving me a sly look.

"We haven't . . . *done it* if that's what you're trying to find out, Jazzy," I replied with a grin. "It's only been a few weeks. We're taking things slow. Getting to know one another again."

"Uh huh," she deadpanned, giving me an eye roll. "I know what you're doing, girl."

I gave her a quizzical, clueless look. "And what is it you think I'm doing?"

"You are keeping that man at arm's length until you figure out how to tell him what it is you do for a living, that's what," she answered, feeling extremely proud of herself by the looks of it.

"Hmph! For your information he knows I'm a freelance photographer. I mean seriously, Jazz? Do you think we've been hanging together for three weeks without the topic of my career coming up for discussion?"

"You know what I mean. He doesn't know the dirty details of your freelancing or you wouldn't have pulled all of your Grace Evangelista shit down off of your bedroom wall. Which also tells me you've got plans for a sleepover here coming up on the agenda," she finished, laughing her ass off uncontrollably.

"Oh, you just know me so well," I replied dryly.

"That I do. That I do. So, at what point will you tell him the rest of it?"

I turned away and tugged one of my pillows over to cover my face. "I don't know. I just don't know," I muttered. "Not until I absolutely have to...or never. Yes, never sounds good."

Jazzy pulled the pillow from my face and gave me one of her no nonsense, stern looks of disapproval. She was really good at those. "You can't put it off forever, Neely. It is, after all, what you do for a living. And you might justify it by saying you told him you're a freelance photographer, but you know as well as I do that by not telling him the whole story is kind of like lying by omission."

"Okay, Jiminy Cricket. Lay off for now. I'll tell him when I know this relationship is going to endure how's that?"

"Whatever, Neely. Come on. Get up and I'll make you some breakfast. And then we can have a nice morning chat like *reasonable people*—is that what you called it?"

"Bitch," I grumbled, tossing the covers back, jumping from my bed, and following my best friend forever out to our kitchen.

Right now I loved my life.

About Andrea Smith

Andrea Smith is a USA Today Best-Selling Author of more than thirty works of fiction. She has a wicked sense of humor, and no matter the genre, she is able to infuse laughter throughout.

Here is a listing of her published fiction to date:
DREAM SERIES
(New Adult Romance/Suspense/HEA)
These Books should be read in order:

ANDREA SMITH

SHADOWS AND DREAMS (Book 1)

"That was definitely hot," I said, propping myself up on an elbow to look at him, "going all 'Christian Grey' on me like that."

"Who?" he asked, totally clueless...

I wasn't prepared for what was in store for me when I took a summer position at Sinclair Stables before my junior year of college. After all, it could only help with my chosen field of equine studies, right?

My first encounter with Trey Sinclair wasn't a pleasant one to say the least. I didn't realize he was taking time away from his law firm in Atlanta to oversee his family's business in Bristol Virginia over the summer. He was definitely an alpha who liked exerting his power . . . and his prowess.

And then there was all this weirdness going on there. Like something from a Hitchcock movie! I was there with baggage I didn't realize I had! Trey Sinclair turned out to be my protector . . . and so much more!

Adult Content. 18+

THESE DREAMS (Book 2)

Think "pink" Mr. Sinclair! There's a new girl in your orbit!

'These Dreams' is the second installment in the *'Dream Series'* and finds Trey Sinclair and Tylar Preston, his fiancée, new parents to an adorable baby girl!

But as their wedding day approaches, Tylar is once again haunted by recurring nightmares that leave her fearful for the safety of her baby. She struggles to unravel her past with the help of a psychologist at Trey's insistence. Together they delve back into Tylar's childhood which opens the door allowing her to secure her future happiness. All is not without cost and there are plenty of surprises along the way.

Their journey together is often rocky with unexpected twists and turns along the way; their passion is relentless. They give each other strength during the difficulties they encounter with friends and family in this continuing story of their love and commitment.

ADULT CONTENT.

SHATTERED DREAMS (Book 3)
Life's About Love . . . And Life's About Pain . . .

My life was about to get even better! Trey and I had a new home, complete with horses for me to train. Preston was growing leaps and bounds; and so happy to have a baby brother or sister on the way. Tristan and Gina had just welcomed their new son into the family.

All was good.

But sometimes life can deal a bad hand or two and you don't see it coming. A sudden loss. A fractured marriage. A separation to clear one's mind or reset priorities. To examine one's heart and soul.

I will always love Trey. Trey will always love me.

But is that enough?

Book 3 in the "DREAM SERIES" is the Author's favorite of the bunch. Read it. You will see why.

DREAM LOVER (Book 4)

Being Tylar's best friend wasn't nearly as easy as I made it look. Keeping my secret past from Tristan was even harder.

Book 4 in the 'Dream Series' is Gina's story.

And it's a surprising one. Maybe Gina isn't the tough cookie she appears to be . . .

My name is Gina Valenti Hatton, and I'm an East Coast girl. I'm Italian, a bit outspoken, and to those who know me, I'm tough as nails.

I live a lie.

There's a part of me that is terrified that he'll find me. And now that I'm with Tristan Sinclair, all thoughts of my past are starting to fade. But Tristan knows I'm keeping something from him, and when my darkest fear shows up, my only hope is that we can survive my past.

It is important to read the three prior books in the 'Dream Series'' prior to reading Book 4.

ALPHAS IN LOVE SERIES
(Contemporary Romance/Suspense/HEA)

Can be read as standalones, but are most enjoyable if read in order.

SLATE (Book 1)

Fate hasn't always served Samantha Dennison well.

A shotgun wedding when she was just 16 years-old to a man who has been cold and distant at best, Samantha devoted herself to raising their only child, Lindsey for as long as she could.

But now, Lindsey is away at college and Samantha can no longer deny her empty life, and doormat existence. At 35, she is desperate to carve out an identity for herself and shoot some adrenaline into her tattered self-esteem. It is with that purpose in mind, she signs up for pole-dancing lessons, never imagining this single decision will change her life forever.

People close to Samantha would never have guessed the soccer mom they once knew could transform herself so flawlessly into the seductive "Diamond," a pole dancer at a Gentleman's Club in Indianapolis. "Diamond" becomes the object of one biker's attention, and as much as she tries not to cross that line, fate once again intervenes, and this time she's fully prepared.

If you enjoy romance, twisty suspense, and second chances at true love, this book will not disappoint!.

ADULT CONTENT

TRACE (Book 2)

Our futures are left to fate. And if we're lucky, sometimes fate throws us a curve ball we couldn't possibly have seen coming.

USA Today Best Selling Author Andrea Smith brings an unlikely pairing in Book 2 of the "G-Man Series."

Nineteen year old Lindsey Dennison returns home after her freshman year of college to find the life she had left existed no more. Her parents' marriage had imploded; her dad was on the run from the law, and her mother had somehow found her lost youth.

All in less than a year's time.

Enter twenty-nine year old Taz Matthews, a sexy FBI agent and partner of her new stepfather, and suddenly Lindsey's life is about to get really complicated.

When Lindsey's safety and well-being are threatened, Agent Taz is sent to protect her. The problem is, there's nobody to protect Taz when he finds himself becoming smitten with the sweet and innocent Lindsey.

Trying to fight the urge proves useless for this hot FBI agent and stuff is about to get real! He finds himself in uncharted territory with Lindsey Dennison. All he knows is that somebody is out to take what he now claims as his . . .

EASTON (Book 3)

Running away from a broken heart, something new to her, the beautiful, privileged and spoiled Darcy finds herself on a far away beach when she sees him.

This beautiful man watching her from down the beach, while he's with another woman. His eyes are only on Darcy. The beginning of something harsh, but extraordinary is about to start . . . and neither one of them will have the power to stop what draws them together.

He is gorgeous.

He is sexy.

He is broken.

He is strong.

He catches her eye in a mirror . . .

Her eyes meet his . . .

She reminds him of someone from his past. And she wants him very much

And it all ***BEGINS***.

ALPHA CRUISE (Book 4)
On the first day of vacay . . .

Spend the holidays with the G-Men, their women and extended family as they cruise the Caribbean in first class accommodations compliments of Easton Matthews!

This book will give the reader an entertaining read, with the usual unpredictable circumstances, along with misunderstandings, love and lots of humor! You will read chapters from each character's point of view, and learn a few things about some of the characters you didn't know.

Along with that, there are bonus chapters, along with a secret "gag" chapter meant only to shock my editor, I promise.

TAZ (Book 5)

"Is he alive?"

USA Today Best Selling Author Andrea Smith brings you your favorite G-Man in this next installment in the G-Man Series!

Trace "Taz" Matthews has it all: a thriving career with the FBI, a gorgeous wife, Lindsey, and two beautiful children. Life doesn't get any better than this for him.

UNTIL one day, when he's asked to temporarily leave his position within the BAU, to handle an undercover mission that is blanketed in secrecy, even within the Bureau. It's a decision he may live to regret when unexpected circumstances cause him to be injured. His injury has far-reaching effects, not only with his life, but with the Bureau, and in particular—his marriage.

You will have all of the suspense, intrigue and steaminess that you've come to expect from . . . Taz.

WESTON (Book 6)

Holy Hockey Puck!

Weston Matthews is 21, a senior in a prestigious, Ivy League College, and has a tongue like Gene Simmons! He's a frat boy, hockey jock, and all around ladies man. He does have one problem though, he has to ace his Early American Lit class in order to graduate and stay eligible to play hockey for Hardwick University.

Weston is provided a tutor to help with his senior Lit class. Enter Penny Lane, also a senior at another local college, doing part-time status at Hardwick. She tutors to earn money, but her aspirations go far beyond just that. Penny is plain, nerdy, brilliant, and has a hidden agenda. She and Weston get off on the wrong foot, and from there, things will only get crazier.

Fasten your seat belts, and hold on for dear life as you take this roller-coaster ride on the Walk of Shame!

BRYCE (Book 7)

Bryce Slater is eighteen. He's a bad boy hottie who has his pick of chicks. He parties a bit. Smokes a little dope now and then. Likes the occasional random hook-up. So what? He's determined NOT to follow in his father's FBI footsteps.

Avery Sinclair is 19. She's in college, and during the summer she works on her grandparents' horse stables and race track as team leader. She takes her work seriously. Her future is in equine operations. She has no time for slackers on her team. But thanks to her uncle doing a favor for a friend, Avery ends up with Bryce Slater for the summer.

"Slater the Slacker" soon becomes Avery's pet name for him, but damn if she isn't determined to whip him into shape. And while doing so, she finds herself inexplicably drawn to him. ***But he's so not her type!***

Bryce Slater quickly gets on the bad side of his new boss, saucy little half-pint Avery Sinclair. She's a sexy little spitfire who is determined to break his spirit. But in the process, Bryce finds himself inexplicably drawn to her. ***But she's so not his type.***

What started out to be a summer of tough love punishment, turns into something both Bryce and Avery never expected. Just as things are heating up, a blast from Bryce's past threatens the fragility of his new found relationship with Avery.

PAPARAZZI

CARSON: THE UNTOLD STORY (BOOK 8)

Sometimes life is just too damned complicated.

I long to stand at the precipice of my existence, watch my whole life replay in front of me in bold, neon, polychromatic flashes from a kaleidoscope that shows my story so I can see how it all finally ends. My aspirations are high, but almost always met. It's the thing I do.

It's who I am, or maybe it is who I *used* to be.

Carson Renee Matthews.

Second child and only daughter of Easton & Darcy Matthews. I've been through an horrific experience, one that left me clinging to life in the hospital. Everyone has questions. I don't have the answers to give them. You see, I have no clue as to the details leading up to my *accident*. But there are people out there that have the answers, and I'm determined to find them - *before they find me.*

Enter Krew Beckett. My former physical therapist who becomes much more than that after he unexpectedly shows up in my life again once I return to campus at Columbia University. But is Krew hiding secrets, or am I simply afraid to trust anyone?

Come take this journey with me.

TRIPLE PLAY (Book 1)
M/M/F ROMANCE W/HEA (Men Series)

Paige Matthews has a lot to learn - about everything, including herself. At age twenty-two, Paige finds herself driving across the country to start an internship with the F.B.I. in Quantico, Virginia.

Having been "pushed from the nest," she is not at all enthused about being under the watchful eye of her older brother, FBI Agent Taz Matthews. She does her best to put things in turmoil, and it isn't long before she finds herself looking for new roommates.

Enter lovers Eli Chambers and Cain Maddox who recently purchased a house and are looking for somebody to help with the bills. It seems as if everything is fitting into place finally for Paige.

Until something happens between her and the guys. The ones she lives with; the ones she loves.

This is no typical "Three's Company" story though. Paige embarks on a journey of self-discovery that teaches her not only about giving, but accepting love as well. She soon realizes that sometimes what you're searching for has been right there with you all along.

DOUBLE HEADER (Book 2)

Will Eli do the right thing, or put their three-way relationship at risk?

This sequel to "Triple Play," finds Paige, Eli and Cain trying to add to their family. Unfortunately, they've been trying for several months with no luck. The stork seems to be ignoring them . . . or is he?

When an unexpected person shows up on their doorstep, it isn't quite the bundle of joy they've been hoping for, but their lives are about to get even more interesting. Someone from Eli's past is about to play havoc with their summer, and put a crimp in their love lives.

Steamy, sexy, and an incredibly complicated scenario is about to play out, that finds Eli caught between a rock and a hard place (pardon the pun).

LIMBO SERIES

(Contemporary Steamy Romance with Paranormal Edge/HEA)

SILENT WHISPER - Book 1

What does a mob capo want with a girl from the sticks?

Everything . . .

For twenty-seven years, I've flitted through life clueless to the God-given abilities that lay dormant inside of me. In the blink of an eye, everything changed more than I ever could've anticipated.

She changed it.

Now I know that nothing is as it seems. I will never be the same again...but this isn't my story.

It's hers.

I'm just being forced to live it, resolve it, and ultimately try to move on after learning that our lives are going to be tangled far more than I would've ever imagined.

My name is Parrish Locke. And I can see the dead.

STOLEN DREAMS (BOOK 2)

I had some dreams they were clouds in my coffee . . .

It's 1974 in Evanston, Wyoming. Cece Adams, a popular cheerleader loves her bad boy next door, Erik Laughlin, a local rocker. They've had their share of ups and downs, but things have turned around for them. They have their dreams after all. And Cece has some news for Erik.

But Erik never gets the news because Cece never arrives at his Valentine's Day gig. There's been a car accident and Cece is dead.

Fast forward forty years . . .

Parrish Locke, a 27 year-old model has only recently discovered she has a gift. It's a spiritual one she sometimes wish she didn't have. It's . . . complicated. But when stalled souls reach out to her, she can't say no to helping them resolve their unfinished business.

Stolen Dreams finds Parrish back in the 1970's, in the small Wyoming town where Cece lived and died as a result of a car accident one snowy night. But Parrish knows this isn't what really happened. After forty years, how will she convince authorities there is more to the story?

One relationship fizzles, while a new one sizzles!

FORBIDDEN SERIES
(New Adult- Taboo/HEA)
Need to be read in order.
CROSSING LINES (Book 1)
When is love wrong?
Jesse Ryan has always been the love of my life, from as far back as I can remember. But time, distance and circumstances beyond my control separated the two of us for many years.

Now things have changed. Because you see now I'm a grown woman, and it's time that Jesse sees that for himself. But will he see me as anything other than the child I was when we last saw one another? It's up to me to make sure that he does.

Look out Jesse Ryan. September is back.

PAPARAZZI

THE LOVE EFFECT (Book 2)

My name is Jesse Ryan. I'm thirty, single, and raising my daughter alone. I'm a construction worker in Arkansas, and in the summer of 2010, I knew I'd need some help with my nine year-old daughter, Scout. That's when September Dawson came back into my world.

She's a beautiful woman now, and a very resourceful one at that. She effectively ambushes a romance that is barely off the ground between me and a neighbor and she doesn't stop there. Suffice it to say by summer's end, I'm hers in every way. Yeah, I get that there's an eleven year age difference, but despite my better judgment and solid resolve, *the heart wants what the heart wants.*

And that brings us to now.

We've managed to keep our relationship discreet, but at the same time, planning our future together. *Then we get . . . the news.* And everything we've been planning is suddenly and inexplicably torn from us. After more six years without a word, my estranged wife, Libby, resurfaces. She has been seriously injured and now suffers from total amnesia. She doesn't remember any of us.

Now decisions need to be made, and everyone looks to me to be the one to make them. But how can I make a decision that will be in everyone's best interest?

SOUTHERN COMFORT
(NA SUSPENSE)

Welcome to Layton, Alabama. Population 11,000. Where the sweet tea runs through our veins, the air smells of cobbler, and the secrets lie so deep that not even the confessionals are safe anymore.

My name is Sunny Gardner. And Layton is my home, or least it had been until Avery Dawson came into our lives. They say that evil comes in all forms, but nobody in Layton expected evil would come to us as a minister who preached the Word, but lived a lie.

This is my story. A story of struggle and triumph and, ultimately, how I saved myself and my community from the devil himself.

Adult Content 17+

EVERMORE SERIES
(NA Romance/Suspense)
This is a 4-set serial of novellas following boy next door first love, through the years to a second chance romance. Must be read in order.
CRUSHED (Book 1)
We were just kids when we met. . .
He was the boy from down the beach.
I was the transplant from Tennessee.
He became my best friend.
I became his best girl.
And then . . . it became us.
We shared things . . . our dreams, our secrets . . . first kisses and then our hearts.
Seth Drake was my everything. My first crush. My first love. My forever passion. Until that day when everything changed through no fault of ours.
I was crushed. We were crushed.

CLAIMED (Book 2)
Love should be everything or not at all.
At least that's what I used to think.

I'm seventeen now, and back in Malibu. Mama's drying out back East, and here I am living with my father and his new wife, Tiffany Blume, Hollywood harlot. At least that's what Mama calls her. I keep my distance. I just have to bide my time until I turn eighteen and go off to college. Away from them; away from Seth Drake.

Seth is living his dream. Studying acting in New York City, landing a recurring role in a hit series, and grabbing my heart one last time until it breaks.

He's got fame. Fortune will likely follow.

I hate him.

I love him.

PAPARRAZI (Book 3)
Chase you till you're mine . . .
"Get ready for your close-up Mr. Drake."
I've found a career. Or maybe a career has found me. It's one I never would have imagined; one that I've never respected. But yes, I am paparazzi now in one of the most flush communities in the country. My reputation is well-known. When the tabloids need the shot, I'm the one that delivers.

I am Grace Evangelista.

I'm really Neely, but a cover is essential in my business. And Seth Drake is about to get up close and personal with my expertise. Is it revenge I want? Or is it simply validation that yes, I can be as good at my craft as he is at his? Whatever the reason, he's about to be blown away. Sometimes the best laid plans go awry for something better.

This just might be one of those times . . .

STAR F*CKING (Book 4)

"Neely, I'm putting my foot down, babe. You are coming with me while I do this film, because there's no fking way I'll be apart from you again."**

Book 4 is the conclusion of the Evermore Series.

Seth and Neely's paths have crossed over the years, but not in the way they had hoped. The misunderstandings between them stem from issues beyond their control, but the truth will be revealed.

No matter who the players are that come in and out of their lives, one thing cannot be denied: Seth and Neely are meant to be together. Their love is destined to endure.

Almost anything.

DREAM SERIES BOX SET

Trey Sinclair always gets his way. That is, until he meets Tylar...

Atlanta attorney Trey Sinclair always gets what he wants whether it's in the courtroom, the bedroom, or on his family's horse farm. But when a bombshell is quite literally dropped into his lap, he can't help but be drawn to the feisty, independent, and strictly off limits Tylar Preston.

But Trey never takes no for an answer and Tylar desperately tries not to break her own rules.

It's only a matter of time.

They both know it.

What they don't expect is their intense and irresistible passion or the danger Tylar finds herself in because of a secret from her past.

Dream Series Box Set is a complete series bundle. Four full-length novels filled with excitement, mystery, and steamy surprises from *USA Today Bestselling Author Andrea Smith.*

Here's what readers are saying:

"I really, *really* loved this series, Andrea just blows me away at anything she writes. But this series is a must read, promise you will not be disappointed!"- **Sammie's Book Blog**

MATURE CONTENT: This story contains sexually explicit material, mature subject matter, and is intended for individuals over the age of eighteen.

Social Media Links:

Follow her on Book Bub:
https://www.bookbub.com/authors/andrea-smith
To sign up for her monthly newsletter, visit her website:
www.andreasmithauthor.com/[1]
Stalk her on Facebook:
www.facebook.com/AndreaSmithAuthor/[2]

---

1. http://www.andreasmithauthor.com/

2. https://www.facebook.com/AndreaSmithAuthor/

Don't miss out!

Visit the website below and you can sign up to receive emails whenever Andrea Smith publishes a new book. There's no charge and no obligation.

https://books2read.com/r/B-A-DYO-GCSLB

BOOKS 2 READ

Connecting independent readers to independent writers.

Did you love *Paparazzi*? Then you should read *Star F*cking*[3] by Andrea Smith!

[4]

*"Neely, I'm putting my foot down, babe. You are coming with me while I do this film, because there's no f**king way I'll be apart from you again."* **Book 4 is the conclusion of the Evermore Series.** Seth and Neely's paths have crossed over the years, but not in the way they had hoped. The misunderstandings between them stem from issues beyond their control, but the truth will be revealed. No matter who the players are that come in and out of their lives, one thing cannot

---

3. https://books2read.com/u/boDAqa

4. https://books2read.com/u/boDAqa

be denied: Seth and Neely are meant to be together. Their love is destined to endure. *Almost anything.* Adult Content 17+
Read more at www.andreasmithauthor.com.

Also by Andrea Smith

ALPHAS IN LOVE
Slate
Trace
Easton
Cruisin' With the G-Men
Taz
Weston
Bryce

Beyond Series
Broken Dreams

Dream Series
Shadows & Dreams
These Dreams
Shattered Dreams
Dream Lover

Evermore Series
Crushed
Claimed
Paparazzi
Star F*cking

G-Man
Carson: The Untold Story

Limbo
Silent Whisper
Stolen Dreams

M/M ALPHAS
Blacklisted
Quid Pro Quo

MMF Sandwich
Triple Play
Double Header

Naughty Nuggets
Santa's Stocking Stuffers

Standalone
Men Duet
Southern Comfort
Dream Series Box Set
Bitch Games: We All Play Them
The Other Man
Wasted
Hard Balled
All of Me
Maybe Baby Box Set
Love in Limbo

Watch for more at www.andreasmithauthor.com.

About the Author

Andrea Smith is a USA Today Best-Selling Author of New Adult Romance, Romantic Suspense, and Contemporary Romance with an erotic tone. She also writes naughty nuggets with Laurel Landon!

Check out her other books! You will never be bored!

Read more at www.andreasmithauthor.com.